AF499363

Sean

The Guardian Angels Pack
Volume 2

Virginie T.

Translated by Feriel Benhamiche

© 2020. T. Virginie

Legal deposit: June 2020

Prologue

I have to get active. I welcome a new nurse today and have been designated to teach her everything. I guess there will have some work to make her fully operational. I have been warned that she is just twenty, so she is an inexperienced novice. She is the age I was when I started this job almost 10 years ago, and I remember very well the obstacles I had to overcome to survive. The days are not always easy to live in this profession.

Damn, I'm a little late, Peter wanted to talk to me before I leave for work. He's the alpha of the Treat pack and my dad. Well, not really, but it's just like. I owe him a lot so when he summons me, whatever the reason, I obey without arguing, like everyone else. He wanted to tell me about the new recruit at the hospital. Like most packs, we have our own geek and Peter do researches about any new people who may come near me. It is painful, but I understand the reasons. He does it for me and Sam. He protects us and I can never thank him enough for his kindness towards us. Fortunately, our conversation was quick, as she is a simple human and therefore poses no danger to us.

So I arrive with only 10 minutes of delay to the service and the new is already there, waiting quietly in the rest room for me to come and get her.

— Hello. You are Sevana, right?

— It's me. You must be the person I was told to wait here.

— Absolutely. My name is Ashley. I will be your most regular colleague on this floor and I am in charge of training you on hospital habits. I prefer to warn you right away, I can be very direct. I say everything I think without a filter, good or bad. I hope you are not susceptible.

— No problem. I prefer honesty to hypocrisy.

— Perfect. So let's go. i'm going to brief you right away, that's how we learn best. Let's start with the first bedroom. I warn you, he's a child with broken bones and lots of bruises. A bad fall on the stairs. He's in a coma, but we're expecting that he will wake up soon. You must not be too sensitive in this job or you will not last long.

— Okay. Don't worry about me. I am sure I can make myself useful.

I like her. She is a volunteer even if she seems shy. I’m sure we’ll get along well over time. I let her read the child's constants while I take the temperature. I am surprised when I raise my head. Why is she holding the boy's hand? Compassion is good, pity no. If she lets herself be overcome by her emotions, she is screwed up.

— You have to be strong, remember? I warned you.

She immediately releases his hand with a start and swings from one foot to the other, uncomfortable. I may be too abrupt. It's only her first day after all. I have been there too and I felt this sadness in front of some patients. We have to stay professional, but we are not insensitive either!

— Do you want to get some fresh air?

—No that's not it.

I am not patient at all. Does she appreciate honesty? Well, I like direct people.

— Stop procrastinating. Spit it out.

She hesitates for a few more seconds before nodding her head.

— The father must be denied access to this room. He must not approach the boy.

I frown at her incongruous request. I did not expect that. Why would we do that anyway? Parents obviously have access to their child's room without restriction.

—For which reason?

She seems more and more embarrassed. She flees

my gaze, hesitant. It doesn't matter, I don't need to hear it to find out what's going on in her head. I open my mind in that moment when she decides to explain it to me.

— I'm not sure he fell by himself. I suspect abuse.

—Why ?

She shrugs without adding anything.

—It's just an impression.

Hmm. Given what is going on in her head, I believe her. The picture of this poor child in a wheelchair, plastered and crying, suddenly pushed in the middle of traffic by his father are violent, and the man is quite recognizable. It looks like he wanted a car to overturn his son. Sevana arrived at the hospital just an hour earlier. It is impossible that she have seen him before. It looks like it's not just me who has secrets. Sevana, if she is clever, she will certainly not confide in me, a total stranger. But I doubt that she has the same protection as me. Peter told me that she lived with a couple of humans. The risks that I will be uncovered are minimal and would undoubtedly be a betrayal. The brunette in front of me probably thinks herself out of danger by posing as a normal human and working in a human hospital, but sometimes we have to treat shapeshifters, Without forgetting the untimely visits of my adopted family. which overprotects me and invades my living space all the time. I can probably help her stay in the shadows and I am sure that she will indeed be able to be useful in this place. She has an incredible talent that I have not seen for far too long. She choosed the perfect profession for her. However, I prefer not to talk to Peter about it. My father can be very suspicious of what he does not understand and Sevana is undoubtedly a real riddle which he would like to question until she cracks. A fatel who appears in the hospital where I work as if by magic will unnecessarily panic the alpha. I would have felt it if she had bad intentions. However, she just wants to help her neighbor. For my part, I mostly found a friend with whom I probably have more in common than I would have dared imagine.

Chapter 1

Sean

I wonder why Connor called everyone so early in the morning. I thought he would like to enjoy Sevana for at least a whole month before resuming our dawn training habits. It has only been a fortnight since he brought his partner back to his house. Note, we didn't see them much during these two weeks, apart from the official pack presentation. Would his desire for the pretty fatel have dried up? No, impossible. The last time I came across them, I had to run away so as not to see them jump on each other in the middle of the forest. Maybe he wants me to take the reins of the Gardian Angels for a while to take full advantage of his wife without having to manage the clan or the governor's missions. We haven't had a call since the Sevana affair, it won't be long before we are contacted for a new assignment. I would understand very well if Connor wanted to free up some time. He is the alpha and has dedicated his whole life to others since he was elected chief, but priorities change when you meet your soul mate and there is no reason why things should be different for him. Especially since Sevana is an exceptional person. She is the last fatel on Earth and has an immense power, out of the ordinary even, a magical power that I had never seen. Always this throbbing pain when thinking of the fatels and their cruel and useless end. I still miss my family so much despite the passage of time, even if the discovery of Sevana has eased my pain. These people did not completely disappear in the end. It gave me hope that others may have survived despite the plots of the dissident packs.

— Is everything right Sean? I feel you agitated.

Hmm, our alpha female, in addition of being very beautiful, and also very perceptive, it is the least one can say. Telepathy is not her main power, however. She can only communicate by thought and not read minds. But she is very observant and has a big heart.

—Yes everything is fine. What is the reason of a convocation by the Great Manitou so early? He is afraid of you and requests the protection of his lieutenants against his own wife?

Sevana has a very communicative crystalline laugh that makes me smile, but also a very possessive guardian angel. Connor places himself behind her back and hugs her, staring at me in an unmistakable gesture for me. My alpha still marks his territory.

Their bond is however sealed, no risk that a person could interfere between them, and their love is deep, but that does not prevent him from being jealous of all males who approach her.

— What did you say to make my wife so happy? It's my role to make her smile.

Sevana turns slightly to rub her nose against his cheek. She quickly learned to tame the cheetah with little attentions. Touch is essential between two soul mates.

— Calm down my teddy bear, he just made a joke.

I explode with laughter when hearing this nickname, followed by Owen, Liam and Nate, who arrived at that moment. Connor groans softly.

— My angel, stop calling me that in front of everyone or no member of the pack will respect me.

— Don't be silly. You are a ferocious plush and everyone knows it.

My hilarity and that of my companions redoubled while Connor bit her earlobe to punish her. Sevana then turns around to kiss him and it is better that I intervene or I will once again be forced to run like a thief so as not to witness their lovemaking, and we will never know why our friend asked us to become. So I clear my throat to let them know we are there.

— Sorry. Thanks for coming guys. I'm going to be direct. I have no time to waste, I want to put my partner back in my bed as soon as possible.

The burning glance that they exchange confirms it to us. It is better that our meeting be short.

— Sevana's friend may be in danger. We need your opinion.

— OK. Let's sit outside and tell us all about it.

The chalet of our alpha is surrounded by table and chairs to be able to gather the whole pack here. So we take a seat around one of them, Sevana on Connor's lap, as usual. These two can't stand not touching each other. I hope to fell this communion of souls one day, like many shapeshifters. Our leader then begins his story.

— Something has been bothering me since we got home and I just find it. Nate, you can give me your impression since you met her. It is Ashley, Sevana's nursing colleague

The bear nods.

— I remember her. A little blonde with green eyes. She had been attacked at the same time as Sevana, but nothing bad.

— Absolutely. And do you remember what she told

us when we met her?

Our friend is thinking. We could almost see smoke coming out of his ears. He is more brilliant for action than for reflection, but he is a faithful friend and a formidable fighter. Better not to be in his path when his beast sets off, a real bulldozer. Ah, it looks like his brain has just started, his whole face lights up.

— She was the one who made us suspect the fatel side of Sevana first . She told us about your partner's extraordinary intuition.

— Exact. But before that, she took her precautions. Before revealing it to me, she asked me if I was ready to protect Sevana, no matter who she was. She insisted on this point.

Nate is more perceptive than I thought.

— Do you think she knew Sevana's origins ?

Okay. I can see what my alpha talks about and it is not good if he's right.

— You think that this Ashley knows about the talent. You think she knows that Sevana is a fatel and that she wanted to make sure you wouldn't hurt her before giving you clues.

— That's what I think, indeed. Sevana and her never talked about it openly, but I think she knew all about her powers, yes.

This could actually become a concern. There is no question that rumors spread among the rebels that at least one fatel escaped the massacre. The fact that the Blacks are aware of this is already sufficiently annoying, even if they will never try anything against us, especially after the heavy losses that we have inflicted on them. However, it could become a problem if several rebel packs hear about it and join forces to destroy us. We have the support of the governor, but in the face of rabid packs, humans can do nothing.

— Sevana, how is your relationship with your colleague?

— She is more than a colleague. She's been my best friend for six years. We're talking about everything, but I'll stop you before you ask me, no, I never made it clear to her that I have intuition, as Connor told you. Anyway, I didn't know my fatel origins. Now she has been my partner for many years, she has seen me work and save lives by alerting symptoms in advance regularly. It is possible that she did guess. But in this case, she never told me about it. In any case, she supported me from the beggining with every alert I gave despite the absence of any obvious sign of deterioration in the patient's condition. She has been my biggest supporter at the hospital since the first day.

I think Connor is right. Her friend must have had

doubts about Sevana, but perhaps, like many, she knows very little about fatels. Their disappearance dates back several years now. Many have forgotten their existence and the new generation has never even known . That’s easy to know.

— How old is your friend?

— 35 years ago.

Okay. They disappeared 25 years ago so she was able to meet fatels as a child and recognize the signs of Sevana's power. I am the same age as her and I remember this people perfectly. At the same time, my childhood surely does not look like hers. In all cases, a legitimate doubt exists. We need to learn more about her before we worry too much. I take my laptop out on the table. I'm not going anywhere without my tool. I’m a geek at heart and the computer scientist of the pack. An ace in my field when it comes to knowing everything about someone.

— Her last name please?

— Ashley Peterson.

OK, let's go. Let the magic of the internet work. I tap for a few minutes on the keyboard and all the information available about Miss Peterson appears on the screen. The record is strangely empty and devoid of photos. A data instantly catches my attention. She’s an orphan, like me. No close relatives are mentioned. Certainly, many of us here have lost our parents, but unlike the others, it happened to me twice, although I don't remember the first one. It is better that I focus on my screen before the rage takes me, as always. Ashley was taken in at the age of ten, but unlike Sevana, not by humans. Ashley grew up in a pack. It's very unusual. Clans that adopt humans are extremely rare. Unless she's less human than supposed?

— No. Impossible. I've already seen her hurt and her wounds weren't healing at high speed like you.

Owen unequivocally confirms this to me.

— And I would have felt it.

No doubt. It would be crazy to put his intuition in question.

— However, she grew up in the Treat pack. The alpha is named Peter Browling.

Liam frowns.

— That name sounds familiar. I heard it somewhere before.

I'm looking at the alpha record.

— It's probably because he's a doctor.

—Probably. It must have been during my nursing lessons.

Probably. Which does not answer our questions.

The mystery is taken more volume, even. I agree with Connor. We cannot remain in the dark. I say out loud what everyone thinks low.

—We have to go and question the nurse.

— I agree. And my goddess could use her talents to see the future of her friend.

The pretty brunette nods, tickling when passing with her long hair, with blue reflections, the chest of her companion. We are silent and remain motionless, our alpha female needs calm to control her power. She has only been using distance premonitions for a short time and it requires a lot of concentration. After a quarter of an hour, she opens her eyes, visibly tired and frustrated.

— Sorry, I can see it, but nothing more. Impossible to see her future. All I can say is for the moment she is fine.

Our alpha female needed physical contact to use her talent until recently. The bond of union amplified her, in addition to giving her access to other powers, but it still requires a lot of efforts and the significant distance between the two people is obviously a obstacle for her perception. It's no wonder she can't do it. That requires practice. Young fatels trained every day from an early age to master their talent to perfection. And as I guess, looking like Connor is upset that he don't want to to seperrate from his wife to go on a mission, I volunteer. As a beta, it’s my job to take over when alpha is unavailable. In addition, I have an advantage over others.

— Okay. In this case, I will go there. She doesn't know me, she shouldn't be wary of me.

Connor supports me, as usual, and he is so happy to stay with Sevana given the smile he has when he looks at her, but he makes one condition.

— OK. It is true that the only time she saw us, we metamorphosed in the corridors of the hospital, we left two dead wolves after our passage, we took Sevana and she hasn't seen her since . It does not build confidence. But you take Owen with you. You may need reinforcement and he knows how to be diplomatic, unlike you.

I nod and we separate on these last words, our alpha already carrying his hilarious companion inside the house. I set off as soon as my mission comrade is ready.

Chaptrer 2

Ashley

I can not believe it. My current rascal boyfriend turned off the alarm last night, because mister wanted to wake up late in the morning. No kidding ? This lazy idiot who doesn't even work reproaches me for waking him with the shrill ringing of my alarm to go to work. It looks like our pseudo honeymoon period we know at the beginning of a relationship is over. Just like our relationship . He will not see me again. Never mind, I will find myself another lover. One who works and does not blame me for not devoting my days to him. In the meantime, I'm late and angry. I run like crazy on the street, jostling a few people strolling their noses up in the air and apologizing lip service without slowing down my race. Concerning politeness, next time, but there, I really don't have time.

I finally get to the hospital, but I'm still 30 minutes late. My department head will blame me again. Especially since we have been understaffed since the attack on Sevana, some nurses having been afraid and given their resignation letter. The bloody scuffle between several shapeshifters on the hospital grounds the following week did not help convince them to return to their jobs. On the contrary, it comforted them in their decision to never set foot in this hospital again, unable to protect their staff. That means I'm going to have to use my charms on this one if I don't want to hear about it for days or take a blame. As expected, I don’t take three steps upstairs without being fired up by a overwrought boss.

— Miss Peterson, you're late. It is unacceptable ! You have no professional conscience? You know, however, that we are understaffed and allow yourself to take your time in the morning.

I take a minute to open my mind and take a deep breath before turning around with my most seductive smile.

— I'm sorry, Mr. Raze. A concern with the alarm clock. It will not happen again.

I spread my soothing waves and my thoughts of kindness to his boiling brain. A priori, I am the third to arrive late today and he intends to make me an example to stop this haemorrhage of latecomers. I'm going to have to force the dose to get out of there. What bad luck ! I will be tired for the rest of the day. However, I don't really have a choice. It is out of the question that I lose my job. I would be forced to return to live in the territory of the pack and I do not wish to see Nathan again for a long time. Not until he finds his partner and stops insisting.

— I'm so sorry, Mr. Raze.

His forehead wrinkles gradually disappear as my power slides inside him. It works well. Humans are so easy to handle. A real child's game that I have practiced from a very young age. Unfortunately it requires so much energy. My boss ends up stammering me, somewhat disoriented:

— It's OK for this time. But don't let it happen again. And let me know about Sevana as soon as you will know something. We miss her very much in the service. She always knew when patients needed emergency care. A true gift from heaven.

I nod my head while going to get change without asking for my rest. I dodged well.

Sevana. She's been my best friend since we met six years ago. I like to chat with her, laugh and cry. She is always there for me, even if I tease her with her nonexistent sentimental life. I never told her about any part of my life, just like she never told me her secret, but she is still my faithful friend. I worry about her. Already two weeks since she literally disappeared. No more traces of her on the surface of the planet. I hope I made no mistake when talking about her talent to this shapeshifter, Connor.

I’ve been protecting her for so many years. Even my family didn't know about her, which was hard to hide. I speak very often of my human friend and Peter works closely with the health services. It was therefore necessary to excel in ingenuity to avoid meeting them on each of his impromptu visits to the hospital. He would never have hurt her, but some members of the pack are not very open—minded, not to say homebody, they do not support new faces, and above all, I know the recommendations of Sevana's parents. She told me about it one day when we had to take care of an animorph, and I didn't want to put her in troubles by making her meet shapeshifters when her family forbade her to associate with them. Maybe I should have, but I thought I was up to the task I set for myself by looking after it. Unfortunately, against the Black pack, I was helpless. I couldn't help her on the day of the attack. I lost consciousness before I even guessed their intentions and tried to intervene. When I regained consciousness, she was already so damaged. These two wolves had literally cut her to pieces. She had suffered so much that hints of fear and pain still floated in her mind, even through her coma. In all objectivity, I could never have put down two animorphs in stride. One, yes, but not two. Peter asked me not to get involved in this story when he heard about the incident. He was very worried about me and I had to convince him that I was in no danger that he would let me keep my job.

When the governor's men came to the hospital, my first reaction was to be afraid for her. I immediately guessed that they were shapeshifters. Their bodies, their muscles and the gleam in their eyes. No doubt possible. I grew up in a pack. I know how to recognize them. But when I got back into the room, they were just looking at her with pity, without animosity. They did not feel what she is, the fault of the drugs injected into her blood. I know the effects of pharmaceutical molecules on the blood of fatel people. Besides, it was better. They could have been scared, angry, or whatever. The disappearance of the fatels is no secret to anyone, unlike the fact that some have survived. And the way the tall brown, Connor, was staring at her when I got back into the room. He was not aware of it, but it looked like there was a connection between them. I have already seen this in animorphs, between two soul mates, but never between an animorph and a fatel. My talent is of little use to me with shapeshifters. Their spirit, inhabited by their animal, is difficult to read, and requires an insane amount of energy to be effective, but I was ready to bet on my life that I could trust him about Sevana. Who would watch over her for me? Now I doubt it. What if I misinterpreted what I perceived? Gene therapy should have already cured her and the Black pack has not re-emerged in the area since she was no longer there. So why didn't she come back? Is she still in danger, pursued by rabid and unscrupulous beasts? Did the Blacks catch and exterminate her the way they wanted, which would explain why the pack was made to be forgotten? Or worse yet, have I given her to monsters wanting to use her? I am well placed to know that certain dissident packs have no limits in killing the fatels. No, some were even more cruel. They captured and sequestered them, using the peaceful members of this people until their death, in endless suffering of course.

When I told Peter about animorphs working for the governor, he was not surprised. He assured me that I didn't have to worry, that the Guardian Angels pack would protect her from all odds. I had never heard of this pack, but my alpha persuaded me that Sevana was safe with them. He is of course not aware of the particularity of my friend, but Peter never lied to me and he was sure of himself. Objectively, a pack that respects human life and fights against rebel animorphs would probably do no harm to a fatel. Besides, I have every confidence in Peter's judgment. He is a benevolent and altruistic chef, even if you don't have to trust appearances. He is the quiet force that possesses the power of a buffalo and the cunning of a hyena. It is better not to be his enemy. Fortunately for me, he is always on my side. Normal, he considers me as his daughter, just like Sam.

The thing that bothers me the most is that I don't know how to contact Sevana and that Guardian

Angels territory is hundreds of miles from here. Too bad, if I don't hear from her by the end of the week, I'll go there and no one will stop me from seeing her. I did some research. It seems that one can enter their territory only by invitation, but I will deploy all my power if necessary to persuade them to let me in and see my best friend, even if I pass out at their door. Once unconscious, they will be forced to bring me in to look after me. And say that I regularly harassed her so that she would go out, meet and open up to the world. She certainly has other priorities today, and her distrust of others has yet to grow. I'm not ready to be able to introduce my family to her. Such a waste !

In the meantime, I take my service by closing my mind to everything around me. It is better. Between the pain of the patients, the anxiety of the visitors and the dirty thoughts of the doctors who imagine us naked under our hospital gowns, I would go crazy if not! It is not always good to know what people think.

Chapter 3

Sean

I hate taking the plane. The expression "feeling like a caged lion" makes sense to me. My pet goes around in my head and demands to be released. I will not have a choice. My feline is far from being docile, it is wild and difficult to control, and feeling locked in a flying tin can for several hours made it mad. It keeps roaring and scratching my skin from the inside to force me to make room for it. It becomes painful and metamorphosing in the city would be a bit annoying.

— Sean, stop snorting, you make the stewardess uncomfortable. They will eventually run away.

Indeed, Owen is right. We wait on the tarmac until our rental car finally arrives and the staff look at me from afar, eyes wide.

— Liam would have loved it. These girls in uniform are quite to my taste. Unluckily he couldn't come. Connor wanted his presence, as well as that of Nate, in the territory to protect Sevana. As if she needed us to defend herself! She is able to kick the buttocks of our enemies just by raising a hand. She is in no danger.

It is true that Liam and Owen are an inseparable duo, both professional and personal. No mistake, however, they are not in a relationship, but they like to share the same partner. Go find out why. I'm more an exclusive type. I want to have a partner who belongs only to me. I must admit that I envy Connor for finding his soul mate. I aspire to find mine one day. But I doubt I can do it. Or at least to please her. I know myself. I am too serious, too focused on my work and the pack. I put everything else in the background, as for my lion, it is aggressive and has no subtlety. It would be able to scare or grumble at our partner, at least. It’s not ideal for finding and winning the love of your life.

Owen gets me out of my gloomy thoughts with a nudge in the ribs.

— Look, there is a wood bordering the airport. Let's free our animals before that you disembowel a human by mistake.

Um, disembowel, my lion's favorite technique. It loves to open its opponents up and down to kill them. For it, it is a clean and fast operation. Animorphs are no secret to anyone, but indeed, some humans, by frequenting us only with our human appearance, forget that we shelter within us a wild and formidable animal, and it would be unfortunate if one of them take a fatal claw spreading his guts to the ground, because he would have made me jump or said a wrong word.

We stop at the edge of the wood, we get undressed so as not to disintegrate our clothes during processing, and let the metamorphosis take place. It happens quickly. The bones snap, the skin stretches, the fur covers us, and I find myself next to a black panther in place of Owen. His animal is superb, all in finesse, unlike my lion which is of a large and imposing stature. I start by shaking my head to snort my thick mane and sniff the air, looking for a possible threat. Beta reflex. Nothing. The smell of the trees around us, moss and bitumen behind me. There are the essence of some animals, but my lion is not afraid of them. I start jogging, enjoying my legs, and play with the ground by planting claws several times. I love the feeling of being one with nature. Owen chooses this moment to jump on my back. Unlike me, he doesn't want to take advantage of this moment to relax, but to let off steam and for that, nothing better than a good fight. It may well weigh less than me, its weight, combined with the fall due to the height of the tree on which it was perched, makes me lose balance by taking my breath away and we roll on the side, legs intertwined. I take advantage of its confusion due to our rolled-up to bite it on the skin of the neck while standing up and I push a fierce roar that makes the surrounding leaves tremble and clear away the rodents nearby. This startles the panther and bristles the back hair. I like to inspire fear in my opponents, even if in this specific case, I know that it is only an instinctive reaction in my pack companion who has nothing to fear from me, but my lion appreciates everything even. I drop my large paw on its shoulder, without taking out the claws. There is no question of hurting my friend, only of beating him up a bit by playing cat and mouse, and I expect Owen to play the role of the mouse. However, the panther does not seem to agree and gives me a kick on the side, scratching me superficially in passing, its claws not being retractable, unlike mine. I roll up my lips against it to tell it of my dissatisfaction and decide to end the fight before finding myself lacerating on all sides, as often happens during our training with Connor and the other lieutenants. To do so, I utter a new cry to destabilize it and take advantage of its momentary disorder to overturn it on its back and grab its throat between my powerful jaw. I don't hug enough to hurt it, but enough to show it who is the stronger of the two of us. The panther stops struggling, feeling my fangs on its chin strap, admitting its submission in front of me. So I release it and resume human form at the same time as him. I thank him while helping him get up.

— Thank you, I needed it.

—You're welcome. Your lion is still on the alert, but I felt that our flight had put it on edge. Can we go now? Will it keep quiet in the car?

—Yes it's good. Let's get dressed and let's go. We've lost enough time and our SUV has arrived.

We make the half hour journey in silence, we focus on our mission. The last time, I did not come to the hospital, I was guarding our territory. Only my alpha and the lieutenants went there. So I don't know how the building is designed and it bothers me. I am a meticulous person, I like to be prepared for all eventualities and there, I have a little the impression to leave blindly. I know who I'm looking for, but I don't even know what she looks like, her folder has no photos. I never even thought of asking my alpha to describe her to me precisely. Too bad, Owen should be able to enlighten me, he was on the last trip here. It would be handy to recognize Nurse Peterson if we saw her in a hallway.

— Owen, can you describe the nurse we are about to interview.

— I barely saw her. You know Connor, he doesn't like feeling trapped in a room with a lot of people. Liam and I left Sevana's room as soon as her friend arrived. I can only tell you that she is slightly taller than Sevana.

— Um, that's not difficult. Our alpha female is as tall as three apples.

— Yes, but she is fierce. It is better to avoid upsetting her.

For sure. From her 160 cm, you could think her harmless. She's the most powerful fatel I've ever seen and she rescued us. I owe her a debt and I hope to pay it off by saving her friend, if she is really in danger.

— You surely remember other things.

— As Nate told us, she has blond hair, but I have no idea how long they were, they were tied in buns, and green eyes. She had pale skin. That, I remember well, because she had a bruise on her temple and it stood out a lot on her white skin.

—OK. A distinctive sign that would distinguish her?

— Sorry, I don't remember anything more. You know I hate hospitals, too many smells for me. It annoys my panther and puts it on edge.

I nod my head. I totally understand. Of all of us, Owen has the sharpest smell, so the fumes of chemical drugs and detergents are a real sensory attack for him.

— No worries, we'll do with it. We will ask to speak to her at reception. The receptionist will bring her to us. It will be simpler than searching the whole hospital. We have just to say that we are her family not to arouse the mistrust of the personnel.

She’s part of a pack after all.

— OK, we do it like that.

Chapter 4

Ashley

This day is endless, a real torture. In addition to my delay this morning which forced me to expend crazy energy, leaving me tired, several patients conditions deteriorated without warning, which makes us bitterly regret all the absence de Sevana, forcing me to run from one room to another to provide vital first aid which, unfortunately, did not save everyone. One of the patients died despite my desperate attempts to keep him alive while waiting for the doctor, also overwhelmed, to intervene. This is not the first time that I have been helpless in face of a patient's illness, but it always lowers my morale, despite the detachment I take from them. I cannot remain indifferent to the distress of the family when they are told that the loved one is gone. And finally, of course I had the daily visit from Greg, who only made my day worse. Since the Black Wolf attack, Peter sends a member of the pack every day to make sure I'm okay, and his daddy-hen side is starting to weigh heavily on me. Especially since the conversation always takes place in the same way, even if I love Greg.

— Hi Ashley.

— Greg. Everything is OK, no attack, you can go back and report.

As usual, he laughs at my frustration. We have known each other since I joined the pack and he is, after Peter, my favorite animorph.

— Don't take it like that. Peter cares about you and doesn't want anything to happen to you.

— You realize that you repeat the same thing to me every day. You are a lieutenant, not a nanny. You have nothing better to do than supervise me?

— It's part of my job. I have to watch over the pack and you're a Treat member so I'm watching over you. And it's always a pleasure to see your dazzling smile.

If I were a shapeshifter, I would groan by showing him the fangs. It would be useless, but it would relieve me.

— OK, OK, I'm giving up. As you can see, I'm fine. You can tell Peter.

— See you tomorrow Ash. Watch out.

I sigh in spite. I'm going to have to talk to the alpha again, but I doubt he will take my complaint into account and since I promised never to manipulate him or the members of the pack, I can not allay his fears.

I barely took a few steps in the hospital when I hear my name through the loudspeakers.

— Ashley Peterson is asked at the front desk. Ashley Peterson.

What happens again ? Maybe Greg forgot to tell me something? I hasten to go to the reception, but don't see anyone I know. There are only two men in the hall, seeming to be waiting for someone. Looking at it, one of them seems familiar to me. I must have seen him before, but I can't remember where. The second clearly draws my attention. A tall, muscular blond. Exactly how I like them. Too bad he is a shapeshifter. I frequent them enough to know that you should never date them, unless you want to be heartbroken, at a minimum. First, because I have things to hide and it's complicated with a man who smells lies at a kilometer, and secondly, because many people wait for their soul mates to make a living and i prefer to avoid myself disillusionment. It's the first time I'm sorry for the rule I've set myself. I would have liked to lick this golden skin by the sun. The two animorphs walk towards me with a determined step, interrupting my contemplation, and the blond speaks.

— Miss Peterson?

— Yes it's me. What can I do for you ?

Where have I ever seen the comrade of this appetizing specimen? Maybe a reunion between packs? Weird. Generally, I don't show myself very much, too risky, although Peter chooses his allies carefully.

— Can we speak to you in private?

That's it, I remember him! The last time, he left Sevana's room with another, leaving me alone with this Connor and the other mountain of muscles. I turn to him suddenly, abandoning the beautiful golden eyes of the blond.

— You! What did you do with Sevana?

I raised my voice without even wanting to, drawing the attention of Alice, the receptionist, to our group.

— Is everything all right Ashley?

— Yes, it's ok Alice.

She continues to observe us with curiosity while picking up her phone. I hope she doesn't call security or I will never have answers to my questions . Now, I want to see Sevana again. The enticing animorph must also worry about the intervention of a third person, because he takes me by the arm manu militari and leads me aside without rushing me, but without leaving me the choice either.

— Could you turn the sound down, please? We'd like to discuss a delicate matter with you. No need to draw attention to us more than reason.

How delicate? Like, your friend is dead and we don't know how to tell you, or like, your friend is far from being ordinary and we know about you? The second hypothesis is implausible. Sevana never knew for me, although the converse is wrong. But the first is simply unbearable for me. I cannot accept the idea that one more fatel has died. I need to be clear heart about this before I go mad at asking myself that way.

— Is she okay?

I didn’t think my voice would shake as much when I said these words, but it’s hard to do otherwise even though my eyes are so wet as the anguish compresses my chest.

— Calm down. She's fine, I promise you.

I could make sure of it by opening my mind, but I'm too exhausted and the amount of energy I should be putting on them would make me lose consciousness, leaving me vulnerable. So I have to believe them.

— What are you doing there? Will she come back and you come to make sure the hospital is no longer under surveillance?

— As I told you, I wish to have this conversation away from eavesdroppers.

That one, glances at Alice, who is still scrutinizing

us despite the people waiting in front of her, desperate to get her attention. I find her behavior strange, she who is usually so picky. So I comply and we head outside the building, away from anyone likely to listen, but in the sight of passers—by, do we ever know.

— What do you want ? Why did you call me?

— Tell us about Sevana.

Very direct and no tact. The beta of the pack, certainly. Nathan is also like that and you can't say I like him. It's not my only problem with him. My annoyance must be visible on my face, as the brown guy tries to attenuate these abrupt remarks.

— Please ? It is important.

It is better to cooperate if I want them to leave quickly. They're starting to make me nervous. And then it will be give and take. I will answer their questions, without saying too much naturally, and they will do the same.

— Sevana was attacked by the Blacks three weeks ago and your friends took her with them a fortnight ago. She hasn't come back here since. I already told your friend Connor everything I know.

— You talked to our alpha, yes.

I tense up a bit. I didn't realize that Connor was the alpha. It is not marked on their forehead after all. He gave orders of course, but they need a leader in an operation and, as a rule, the alphas rarely leave their territory. I thought Peter was the exception that proves the rule. I was wrong. Hopefully it was my only mistake.

— Don't worry. As I have said, Sevana is in top form. Our alpha will never hurt her. I even feel sorry for the madman who will try to make him do it. Your friend is far from helpless.

I do not understand. Sevana is the most adorable person I know, she wouldn't hurt a fly so what does that remark mean and their smiles heard? Would their alpha be ready for any sacrifice to help her? Why would he do that? Because of the bond that I perceived between them?

— Your sense of honor is remarkable if you are ready to die for her. After all, she's just a little human.

The tall blond frowns dissatisfied. Looks like I offended him.

— Don't take us for fools please. I hear your heart panic every time you leave out information.

The disguised lie remains a lie.

I see. It will be difficult to cheat them. But I can be derogatory too if he takes it like that.

— Don't insult me when you haven't even told me your names or why you are here.

The two stooges look at each other and it's the brown who breaks the ice. He is definitely the more diplomatic of the two.

— You are right. Sorry. We're civilized shapeshifters normally, but when it comes to our ...

— From Sevana, we are on our guard.

I could swear that the brown guy meant something else, but the blond cut him off by glaring at him. Our what? What does Sevana represent for them? A prisoner? The brown resumes without formalizing the intervention of the beta.

— My name is Owen and this is my beta, Sean. Now that the presentations are made, can you be honest with us?

— You told Connor about Sevana's intuitions. What do you know?

A real beta, no tact. He just waits for us to execute, that's all. But I'm not ready to betray my friend for his beautiful eyes. Even if these eyes are really bewitching.

— I said everything I knew last time. Sevana has intuitions, of course, but that's all. He is an exceptional person and you must protect her.

—This is what we do. But our alpha couple is worried about you.

Their alpha couple? It looks like I misinterpreted

Connor's look on Sevana as well. He is already linked to a woman.

— There's nothing to worry about. The Blacks didn’t go after me, I’m an insignificant person for them. And anyway, I am not without support. My family watches over me.

— The Treat are powerful, for sure. But are they ready to risk their lives for you?

They did researchers about me. That does not surprise me. No problem, the geek of Treat cleaned on the net when I joined the pack. There is nothing to discover on my file, he made sure of it.

— You are well informed. Yes, the Treat pack is very attached to the little human that I am. Tell Sevana to call me as soon as possible please. And now, excuse me, but patients are waiting for me.

I quickly turn around to resume my service before the interrogation resumes. It didn’t go as I expected. Sevana is safe, I don't think they lied to me on this point, but I don't know anything more and I was afraid to say too much and endanger her. Maybe she found a way to hide her secret? It is not very probable, but not impossible. I am the proof. Besides, Sean makes me feel strange things and I hate what I don't understand. I don’t want to fall in love with an unfriendly shapeshifter who obviously doesn’t interest me. Not that it matters. I'm going to immerse myself in work to remove this sexy vision from my head and everything will be for the best. As for my plan to join Sevana with the Guardian Angels, I have to weigh the pros and cons. The pack is already inquisitive far from its territory, so if I go to their place, I dare not imagine their insistence on getting answers to questions that I refuse to talk about.

Chapter 5

Sean

This little nurse leaves a very strange impression on me. She's very sexy, that's undeniable. A pretty blonde with sparkling and bewitching green eyes. When she fixed her gaze on me, a whole series of images of her under me, in different positions, crossed my mind. Her pretty voluminous breasts that stretched her blue blouse and her beautiful smooth and thin legs awakened my wildest fantasies. I saw myself carrying her to my bed, her legs around my waist. Only when I inspired, all my hopes fell apart at once. With such an epidermal reaction, such as I have never felt before, I dreamed for a moment that she was my partner, and her smell wiped out my nascent happiness. Her smell was bland, strange even, under the stench of the hospital, without any interest, and made my lion frown that curiosity in front of this female had aroused. Owen takes me out of my gloomy state.

— What do you think ?

— She knows more than she says.

My friend nods.

—I agree with you. She hides things. And her smell is weird too.

There, I'm interested. Owen's flair is legendary. Perhaps he has succeeded to determine what makes her smell odd and uninteresting.

— How weird?

— Didn't you notice anything?

— I found it bland, erased.

Owen tilts his head to the side and looks at me more closely.

— You seem to be disappointed.

I don't want to go any further now. The pack above all.

— No, I'm just frustrated to have met a wall.

— If you say so. In short. To get back to her smell, I was attacked by the smell of the hospital, as always, but then I perceived her smell, but it was as attenuated, you are right, and it changed constantly.

I am confused. It does not make sense. Our smell is registrated in our DNA. It never varies, from our birth to our death. Owen shrugs, probably following the same reasoning as me.

— I know, it doesn't make any sense, but I'm sure of myself.

I would never question Owen's words about his flair, but suddenly the mystery deepened around nurse Peterson. The beautiful blonde is intriguing me more and more and I do not like to get interest on her beyond measure. It is not my destiny and I must focus on my mission.

— What do you want to do now? Are we going home?

Good question. I have a feeling that we have to stay here. And it is not the receptionist who fixes us behind the glass door of the entrance that will contradict me. I didn't think that the presence of animorphs still attracted attention. I feel like an animal in a zoo.

— Let's get out of here and wait for the nurse to finish her shift. I want to know the end of the story before I return to the territory. And it's better to make sure she's not afraid of anything before coming home. I do not wish to undergo Sevana's anger.

Owen laughs out loud.

— Does she scare you?

— A little yes. And you should be wary too. She has become formidable.

As agreed, we waited until the end of the day while being discreet. We naturally called the alpha couple to keep them informed and they renewed their confidence in my judgment. They both assured me that I should stay put as long as my gut dictates. For the moment, my instinct is at half mast, I don't feel much except for the nervousness of my feline and how it is focusing on the beautiful Ashley. It who had calmed down with the fight with Owen after leaving the plane has been tense again since meeting the female. It is like in bad mood. It growls and fidgets in all directions, without trying to materialize. It looks like, like me, it doesn't know how to react to the pretty blonde.

We are posted in front of the hospital parking , so that we can see her go out and be able to follow her without being spotted. We want to talk to her and get the real answers to our questions this time. She does not live on the territory of the pack, even if she is not very far from it, and the best would therefore be to question her at home, in her environment which will reassure her. I start to get impatient when my phone rings in the passenger compartment of the car, startling Owen, dozing in his seat.

— Sean with you.

— Sean, listen to me carefully. Are you still in the hospital?

I sit up on my seat, on the lookout. Sevana's voice is rushed, anxious. There is something going on.

—Yes. Tell me everything.

— There is a problem. I no longer perceive Ashley.

— What do you mean ?

— Until then, I couldn't see her future, but I knew she was fine. Now I don't feel anything, nothingness.

OK, that is not a good sign.

— What about Owen and me? Did you try?

A silence answers me. I guess she didn't think about it with the stress and she's trying right now.

— Go to the parking behind the hospital. Three wolves with Ashley.

I don't take the time to listen to more. I shake Owen and run off to the parked cars. I quickly spot Ashley, in the middle of a conversation with men, her hand on the door of her car. They must have approached her as she prepared to go up there. I prefer to slow down and not rush, in case she knows them. I position myself a few meters away, panther on my heels, against the wind so as not to be spotted, but ready enough to be able to follow what they are saying.

Fortunately, the hearing of shapeshifters is better than that of humans. This allows me not to miss anything that turns out to be an dispute.

—Where is your girlfriend ? Can you contact her?

— I don't see who you're talking about. I have a lot

of friends.

— Don't make fun of me human. You might regret it like your colleague. It is said that she was delicious.

Ashley winces in disgust when my lion shows fangs.

— I don't know where she is.

— Yet the Guardians came to talk to you. What did they want with you?Well. Looks like news goes fast here. However, I didn't feel any shapeshifters around when we were with Ashley. No one was monitoring the establishment. You have to believe that they have an indic who went unnoticed.

— I don't know who you're talking about. There was Greg, a member of the Treat pack, who visited me today. You must have confused.

Another half—truth. The nurse is smart, but that may not be enough. The Blacks, I am convinced that they are the ones, are starting to lose patience in the face of their blatant lack of cooperation. The older man grabbed her by the arm, rolling up his lips. From here I see his fangs getting longer. The situation could quickly escalate.

— Don't lie. The receptionist saw them. Where is Sevana Slat? On their territory? Are they planning to bring her back here?

Of course, the receptionist a little too curious. I

should have known. She spies on behalf of the Blacks. Ashley winces under the pressure on her arm, but doesn't give an inch. She's really a loyal friend. I find it admirable. She is used to shapeshifters, but it takes courage to oppose an angry dominant male.

— You'll never catch her. Whatever you do to me, I will not help you.

I get transformed at the moment the wolf raises his hand to hit her. My lion took control without having time to intervene. Still, I should have wanted it. I attack the first wolf who tries to intervene as soon as he sees me, discerning in my peripheral field of vision that the panther of Owen does the same with the second. The fight is fast and flawless, my feline opened the canine without having an ounce of hesitation, from the neck to the stomach. Owen, on the other hand, cut its throat. During this time, Ashley has managed, surprisingly, to free herself from the third one, which now seems confused. He looks at his colleagues without really seeing them and ends up crashing to the ground after having staggered over a few steps. What just happened? Owen shakes his head sneezing, as if to chase something, while my lion yells at me to sniff the air. I vaguely smell something in the air, but don't take more time to discern where it comes from when I see Ashley's eyes roll back. I barely have time to jump forward before she collapses on the back of my inert lion. The king of the savannah, so ferocious in normal times, begins to groan pitifully in my head while laying down gently on the ground, the woman always on him. Owen returns to human form to come and help me. He gently raises the nurse and puts her by my side, allowing me to regain control. My lion is no longer of any use anyway, it is very disturbed, go figure out why. It's the first time that disemboweling someone hurts it.

I see no injuries on the nurse and her breathing is regular. I don't understand why she lost consciousness. Maybe she was very scared and passed out? I don't know and I regret the absence of Liam, our doctor.

— Let's move on. The last wolf just passed out and I have enough blood on me.

— OK. But we take the girl. Connor is right. She is in danger. Even if she doesn't know the origins of Sevana, she is her friend and this is obviously reason enough for the Blacks to go after her.

Owen sketches a gesture to carry Ashley, but the idea of knowing her in his arms disgusts me. So I rush to grab her before him and pass him under his surprised gaze.

Chapter 6

Ashley

I knew I was too exhausted to handle this wolf, but it didn't really give me a choice. It was literally starting to grind my arm and I didn't want to take a hit that would have caused a new bruise on my face. Peter and Greg are sticky enough without that. They would have been able to assign me a permanent bodyguard. The intervention of the Guardian Angels' animorphs was a perfect diversion so that my assailant would not notice anything. The mind of the shapeshifters is already complex, but if in addition, the animal in them perceives the breaking of power in their head, the talent becomes useless. Fortunately for me, this stupid wolf was too busy with the surrounding fighting and offered no resistance. Unfortunately, I got exhausted and lost consciousness. Which probably explains why I find myself in an unknown room. Positive point, I am alone in bed and always dressed. Negative point, I don't know where I am or with whom. Because there is one who is certain. I certainly didn’t come here alone and I can hear muffled voices from across the door. Peter is going to be sick of it when he learns about the attack and I'm not about to get rid of Greg. The alpha is not about to leave me in peace and may even demand that I come back to live in the territory of the pack. I never told him why I decided to move and I don't really want to do it now, but a homecoming is unthinkable, because the reason that made me leave at that time is still valid today.

Well, I have had enough rest. Let's face my saviors. Unless they are my next executioners. Okay, i don't think so. I am neither tied nor gagged and the door opens easily when I turn the handle. I put my head in the doorway and fall nose to nose or rather nose to torso, with Sean. I jump back in surprise and painfully look up from his well—drawn, tanned abs that I want to follow with my tongue to fall on his mocking gaze. Caught in the act of admiring. Never mind.

— Hello.

— Hello. Come eat. You need to gain strength. You were unconscious for a long time.

Ouch. I completely drained my energy in front of them. It really could have put me in danger. However, I learned years ago to manage my abilities, but I clearly let myself go.

— How long have I slept?

— A whole day.

Shit. Peter will kill me. After launching the whole pack to look for me, of course. I absolutely must call him before the situation turns to disaster. I don't want to be responsible for a war between packs. However, my alpha must already be aware of my altercation with the Blacks since there are corpses of wolves in the parking lot of the hospital. And if, in addition, he hears of my conversation with the Guardian Angels, it risks creating a hell of a mess.

— I have to call.

The beta shakes his head in denial.

— You have to eat before you have a syncope. And you still owe us an explanation.

So that's why they were still there. I'm stung on the spot.

— I don't owe you anything at all. Who do you think You Are ?

His face contracts and his eyes sparkle.

— We saved you so it's give and take. If you want your butt to be safe, you're going to tell us everything you know about Sevana.

Damn it. It’s a shame that I’m not able to use my talent. I would have given him the ideas in place to Mr. muscles. Owen intervenes by positioning himself between us before I i get mad. Wise decision.

— We both calm down. Ashley, for the moment, you're our guest. I prepared you something to eat. Come and sit down please. Sean, go for a walk. I can feel your animal fidgeting from here.

Sean chattering teeth for me before rushing through the door. Is he serious there? He thinks he scares me? I have lived in a pack full of dominants most of my life. This guy is so cute, but behaviorally, it really ruins everything. I feel sorry for his future partner.

I follow Owen to the table where a plate of grilled bacon and tomato with beans is waiting for me, accompanied by steaming coffee whose aroma makes me salivate.

— Eat, please. I can hear your stomach from here.

Indeed, my stomach loudly manifests that it has been empty for far too long. I throw myself on the food and devour everything in a few minutes under Owen's inquisitive gaze.

— Do you feel better?

— Yes thanks. That was delicious.

He clears the table then takes a seat in front of me. Here we are. The interrogation will start again. Only this time, I'm in good shape and I too will be able to have information, even if it means having to look for it in my head, if necessary. Then I could take care of Peter before a shapeshifter war breaks out and reveals the greatest secret in history.

— Would you like to talk now?

At least this animorph is diplomatic. Not like his cute and intriguing teammate with whom I would like ... no, but it's not okay. Where did these ideas come from? I smack my mind for my stupidity and focus again on Owen who watches me without connecting.

— As long as it is reciprocal.

— I agree. I will answer your questions as long as they don't endanger my pack. We start?

OK. It is acceptable. The Treat pack would do exactly the same. Nothing should take precedence over the security of the clan. I therefore launch hostilities.

— Where's Sevana? How is she ? Why doesn't she come back?

He shakes his head making fun of me.

— It's been more than one question. We'll take turns if you don't mind. Already, I reassure you, as we have already told you, yes, Sevana is doing wonderfully.

— Why would I believe you?

— We'll call her at the end of our conversation if you want to.

Right answer. I will only know by her voice if all is well.

— Very good. What do you want to know ?

— Let's start with something easy. How did you meet Sevana?

— At the hospital. I oversaw her training and we became friends. Where is she ?

— On the territory of my pack. What do you know about Sevana?

— She was adopted by humans when she was a baby. She is intelligent, beautiful and unique.

He tilted his head to the side and looked at me more intensely, his eyes taking the shape of those of a feline. I see. It's his animal that measures me. I couldn't pay attention in the parking . I have clearly distinguished a black panther and a lion, but it is impossible to know which of the two species it belongs to. As much to ask, it will be simpler.

— What animal are you?

— A black panther.

So Sean is a lion. It fits him like a glove when i think about it. After all, he roars as much as the beast.

— Tell me about Sevana's intuition.

— I haven't asked my question yet.

— Of course you did, you asked me what species I belong to.

I remain motionless for a moment. He's right, but I didn't think it counted as a question. This man is clever and somewhat devious. And I don't know what to answer to protect Sevana.

— You think too much. Be honest. It was the deal.

— Sevana always knows when a patient is going to need help. She is an excellent nurse.

— We already told you, half a truth is considered half a lie. I hear your heart speeding up. What are you hiding from me?

He knows I'm not saying everything, but nothing can force me to betray my friend.

— Nothing. She never told me how she knew.

— Exact. But you know it even so.

Sean arrives at this moment and I thank the sky for it, because I was trapped alone. If I lie, he will know, and if I tell the truth, I put Sevana, who is at the home of shapeshifters, in danger. In any case, I'm stuck.

— So she's talking?

— Her heart speaks more than she does, but yes. She knows everything.

—Good. So she comes with us.

Am i dreaming or these two talk about me like I'm not there? And it is out of the question that I follow them wherever it is without knowing where, although following this beautiful blond in his bed crossed my mind for a moment when I saw him there, sweaty, his tee— shirt sticking to his skin.

—Hey. I'm here. I have my say, right?

Sean turns and looks at me hard, devoid of emotion.

— You know what Sevana is and I'm ready to give my life for her. Now the biggest danger hanging over her is you and what you know. So you come with us.

— Would you give your life for her?

He pursed his lips, but did not answer me. He said more than he obviously wanted. So I open my mind to understand what he refuses to tell me. In his mind, there is only that for his alpha under a layer of anger. It's strange and it hardly advances me, but I prefer to withdraw before his lion spots me.

— What did you do ? Your smell has changed again.

I look at Owen who stares at me, intrigued. I was unaware that my talent influenced my essence. Maybe it's due to the drugs? I'll have to talk to Peter about it.

— I don't know what you're talking about.

— Stop lying. Owen is a fine bloodhound, he never makes mistakes.

He's starting to annoy me with this beta. Why is he so angry? I didn't understand the reason. But I can be kind too.

— Take me home immediately.

— Listen to me, little blonde. Sevana is a fatel, you know it, just like us, and you are going to follow us to protect you, because the Blacks also know and you are their only means of pressure to reach her.

I am amazed. So they really know. And they protect her anyway. I am aware that there are good packs. Treat is one of them. But to protect the fatels is to risk being exterminated by the rebels. There must be a good reason for this. I want to know theirs.

— Why are you protecting her?

Definitely, Sean is stingy with answers. Fortunately Owen is more open.

— We have nothing against the fatel and Connor cares more for her than for his own life.

— Connor, your alpha? You told me he was in a relationship. I do not see…Oh my God, I understand. I was right, there was a connection between the Guardian chief and Sevana. I never could have imagined that.

— She is your alpha female.

— Yes, and now let's go before the Blacks fall on us.

He annoys me with his dry tone of a little chef who accepts no reply. Is that what makes him angry?

— Sean,are you disturbed having a fatel as an alpha female?

Finally a smile from him. And damn it, what a smile. He is even more beautiful with relaxed face.

— On the contrary, it is a great honor.

He exudes sincerity. This man is an enigma for me. No time to dwell on this, I remind Owen of the terms of our agreement.

— I would like to speak to Sevana now.

Out of question to override our agreement.

Chapter 7

Sean

What else is this story?

—Why ?

The pretty nurse squinted her magnificent green eyes, turning her gaze to me.

— Because this is the deal I made with the panther. I answered questions and then we called her.

She has a knack for getting me out of my hinges. Her stubborn and rebellious character excites and horrifies me at the same time, and let's not talk about the effect she has on my lion which scratches me and growls. However, the olfactory attraction is not and it puts me and my animal even more on edge. But if I want her cooperation, I will have to make efforts or she will not get on the plane of her own free will. And if she comes up with a bump on her head because I knocked her out, Sevana will kick my butt, or worse. The fatel revenge could be very painful.

— I'm going to call Connor to keep him posted and

if Sevana agrees, you can talk to her.

— And why would she refuse to speak with her best friend?

I growl in frustration. She pisses me off at having everything answered. To believe that she must have the last word at all costs. And at the same time, she burns with the most exciting interior fire. I prefer to take a few steps away before I bite her in retaliation. I doubt she will take it well, even if the idea tempts my lion.

— Connor? Ashley woke up.

— Good. Did she tell you anything?

—You were right. She knew about the power of Sevana.

—How?

—No idea. And this girl is more stubborn than a mule.

Ashley hits my arm, making me dark eyes.

— Stop pretending I'm not here, it's annoying. And pass me Sevana. I want to talk to her now!

I hear the alpha couple laughing through the telephone when my alpha exclaims:

— It looks like this girl is not afraid of you. Didn't you do her the bad beta who commands?

He laughs at me ? And my little blonde reaching for

the phone, stamping her foot. Hold on. My little blonde? No, she's not mine and never will be. I put the speaker on before she pounced on me to snatch the telephone from my hands, her chest pressing against me, rekindling my untimely desire for her.

— Sevana? You're okay ?

— I'm very well Ash, don't worry about me.

— Obviously I was worried. The last time I saw you, you were seriously injured and in a coma.I see tears beading in the corners of her eyes and I realize how much anguish she has felt since the attack on her friend. I can't help but gently stroke her back to comfort her while she continues to chat. I can't resist to touch her.

— Little secretive. You could have called me to tell me that you had been kidnapped by a beautiful alpha male who wanted to put you in his bed!

Connor laughs back at her as I hear Sevana choke on her saliva.

— I'm really happy for you sweetie. Doesn't your Connor

I tense up at the image that crosses my mind. The idea of Ashley in the arms of a member of my pack, or even two, if it is Owen and Liam, is unbearable to me. I instantly withdraw my hand from her back, as if I had been burned. After coughing several times to catch her breath, Sevana resumes her seriousness.

— Ash, the Blacks are going to chase you. Come join me, you will be safe on Guardian territory.

— Sorry, but I can't leave ...

— I need to discuss certain things with you and we can't do it over the phone.

Ashley sighs and lets a silence settle.

— Please Ash.

— Okay. Give me a few days and I'll join you.

Sevana lets out a shout of joy so stridently on the phone that the nurse is forced to move the handset away, but her smile leaves no doubt about the joy she feels at seeing her friend again. I would like her to look at me and smile at me that way, but facing me, she just pursed her lips.

— Passe us Sean please. And do me a favor, you want. Do whatever he asks you to do.

— You have no right to ask me that. He is a killjoy, overbearing and ...

— Ash, you have no choice.

She gives me the cell phone, muttering I don't know what obscenity without even looking at me. Hearing her say what she thinks of me leaves a taste of ashes in my mouth and my bruised heart. As for my lion, it completely fell back on itself.

— Sean, can you hear me?

I clear my throat and shake myself.

—Yes I'm listening.

— The Alpha in the Treat pack contacted me. He learned about the attack at the hospital and is very upset. Accompany Ashley on their territory, he wants to be sure that she has nothing, and discuss with him. We must make sure that he is able to protect her if she refuses to stay with us.

I don't want her to join the Guardians. Having to watch her while keeping my distance will be beyond my strength, and yet I have a lot. And I have no desire to see her flirt with others.

—Don't worry. I will prepare them to face her return.

— Aside from that, are you all right?

— Of course. Why this question ?

— Owen told me that your lion is very restless.

The joys of living in a pack and getting to know each other so well. We can't hide anything from anyone.

—I manage. I'll keep you posted as soon as possible.

When I hang up, I see that the object of my torment is no longer in the room.

— She's in the shower.

Wonderful. Owen has noticed my confusion, but in addition, from now , I will spend my time visualizing Ashley, naked in the shower, the water streaming in her thick hair the color of the sun, to end up stranding on her splendid lower back . I'm just getting my erection just thinking about it. I have to get out of there before Owen notices.

— I'm going to run my lion. Get ready and let our guest know, we're going to the Treat.

My lion is literally mad. It is bruised, although it has no physical injuries. It claws the surrounding trees at full height, planting its nails deep in the surface of the wood, runs out of breath with no specific destination, and roars repeatedly like a dying wild animal. After half an hour, I finally manage to regain control over it and get transformed into pain as my lion fights against me. I get dressed and can only see the damage it has caused. All the trees are devoid of bark, the ground has been completely turned upside down by its claws and my head still reasons with its howls. It's high time to run away before being arrested for nocturnal noise. In addition, the night partly camouflages my work, but when sun will raising up, it will be another story. The neighbors may be afraid and shoot me. Discretion side, we can forget about.

I just pass my head in the half-open of the front door to shout:

— We're taking off.

I leave without delay and start the car, ashamed of the behavior of my animal and more angry than ever against myself and my attraction for the beauty that I see leaving the house.

Owen is not fooled and his raised eyebrow, accentuated by his mouth open in O, indicates to me that he noted the carnage. He's kind enough to say nothing and we take the road as soon as Ashley is comfortably seated in the rear, prominently displayed in my rearview mirror.

Chapter 8

Ashley

I'm more than confused about the dementia crisis, there's no other word, from Sean. He is completely going crazy outside and lost control of his lion, trashing everything in its path, a real massacre. A magnificent lion, by the way. An imposing beast of at least 200 kg, with well-drawn muscles, a hair the color of hot desert sand and a thick mane in which I would have liked to slide my fingers to know if it is also soft that she looks like. Finally, in other circumstances, because given the fury which the animal displayed, it was better not to approach it if we held a little bit to life. I tried to calm it down, but I couldn't even touch it mind because of the rage taking over. The betas are however chosen for their usual self control. Sean may have a mask of coldness, but I know by now that he is bubbling inside with intense and devastating fire.

The travel to the territory of the Treat pack is made in a heavy and uncomfortable silence. Sean's hands clenched on the steering wheel, making his knuckles white, proof that his tension has not yet subsided, although his tightly contracted square jaw was already a clue in itself, and Owen regularly glances at him furtively , indicating that he is probably as worried as I am about his friend's unstable behavior. It's encouraging ! We are approaching my home and I must absolutely intervene or the meeting with Peter will inevitably turn into disaster. An animorph cannot appear in front of an alpha in such a nervous state unless they have a very strong desire to fight. My adoptive father can only take his state of extreme restlessness as a challenge. However, Sean may well make me made, I don't want him to be hurt, any more than Peter, who has done so much for me and for Sam. Sam… I'll take the opportunity to go see her and make sure her condition is stable. I'm worried about her even if Peter takes care of her and keeps me up to date. She has not had a crisis for several weeks, a real improvement. I hope this time her mental stability will be lasting. Come on, enough self—pity. I absolutely must defuse the situation before we enter Treat territory.

— I should call Peter to notify him of our arrival.

— No.

I feel irritated every time Sean opens his mouth. That is a pity because his deep, almost rocky voice makes me feel like an ox and his lips could be used for better skilful. I pinch my lips and resume as calmly as possible.

— It's an alpha meticulous about the protocol. It is better to announce our arrival if you want to meet him in good condition.

— He already knows. He and Connor chatted by phone. Your alpha is waiting for us.

I recline into my seat. I don’t know what the two Alphas said to each other, but I doubt Peter told him about my secret and Connor would certainly not endanger his partner. I can't believe Sevana is linked to a shapeshifter! She who fled them like the plague, she now lives among them, with their leader. Unbelievable. But this is not the subject. I have to manage to divert Sean's attention from what is bothering him.

— Can we stop at my house before we go see him? I would like to get changed.

—Why ? A male to impress?

Enough is enough. There is enough of diplomacy.

— You can't talk without groaning at the end! I've had the same clothes since yesterday morning, I stink!

Owen calms the atmosphere before the situation worsens again between the beta and me. I always feel like I'm walking a tightrope in his presence.

— We'll pass, no problem. It's on the way anyway. But hurry up. I would like to be there before dark and the sun is already setting.

The two shapeshifters take a huge place in the middle of my apartment which seems suddenly, small, skimpy. My living room seems tiny with two men of their corpulence in the middle who are bigger than my sofa. And what is this habit of sniffing everything like that? It looks like two dogs smelling a bone. They keep looking at each other, like communicating in silence, and inhaling again. Sean finally stared at me, his eyes the color of molten gold. His lion is among us and his eyes are intense to say the least.

— Do you live with someone?

—No I'm single.

He shakes his head, unhappy.

— A woman, a roommate?

—Absolutely not. What is it again ? You start to growl again, it's painful.

Owen puts a hand on his shoulder to calm him down and invites me to go and change without paying any more attention to them. I do so while leaving the door to my room slightly ajar. This allows me to undress in privacy while spying on their conversation for the less informative.

— Sean? It's okay ?

— Do you feel it ?

— Yes.

What do they smell? My home is nothing special and I wash it regularly so what interests them?

— Has Sevana already come here?

— Not for a long time even if it is. It cannot be her. After three weeks, you wouldn't feel anything.

What does the smell of my apartment have to do with Sevana? I must know. I open my mind and direct my power towards Owen, who seems more accessible to me. Damn! Magic !!! I instantly withdraw in surprise. They breathed hints of magic. What a negligence of my part.

Obviously, I take far fewer precautions at home since I never invite anyone. A priori it is wrong. And this will raise even more questions from them. Wonderful. I hurry to finish and join them as if nothing had happened. Owen is watching me, but Sean is nothing compared to him. He examines me with even more intensity than before and a wild gleam dances in the depths of his feline eyes. The king of the savannah is more present than ever and I could literally catch fire in front of his glowing glance. I clench my legs and walk in the door before they feel my uncontrollable excitement. This man really has an undeniable effect on me and I find it disturbing, because his behavior leaves something to be desired! On the other hand, if he manages to ignite my senses with a simple glance, I dare not imagine what it would be like if he touched me! I would probably liquefy immediately.

Chapter 9

Sean

The smell of cinnamon and lime, both fresh and spicy. My lion dreams of rolling in it. Of course I felt the magic, like Owen, but this feminine and assertive smell far surpassed it. As Owen didn't mention it, I guess it doesn't matter to him, unlike me. It’s the scent of my partner, I’m sure. A shapeshifter could never be wrong on this point. Ashley assured us that she lived alone and I am sure she did not lie. Her heartbeat had no variation. So that’s her personal essence. She is in perfect agreement with the visual feeling that I had the day I met her. This gorgeous, luscious blonde is my soul mate, I finally found her. It remains to be found how she camouflages her delicious fragrance and where the magic we detected comes from. The two questions are probably linked. My delicious partner is an enigma that I dream of solving, among all the other ideas that she inspires me and on which I prefer not to approached in the presence of a third person, because it could become annoying. But most of all, I must be forgiven. I behaved like a moron, a dominant beta male in all his glory, dictating my law as a dictator, and I noticed that she took it the wrong way every time. As I thought, my character puts my half off and I know in advance that it will be difficult for me to change, but I am ready to try for her. I hurry to join her and open her door just before she reaches it. She looks at me, destabilized, and gets into the car without saying anything. I lead us to Treat territory, lost in my thoughts, but infinitely more relaxed since I understand my attraction to my passenger. I wonder how I will be able to win her confidence, and her heart at the same time. I'm not good at it. My pack has always been my priority, the missions that we carry out have a particular value for me. Today I have to forget my past and my anger to make the woman of my life happy.

The territory of the Treat pack is very secure. A fence of 2.5 meters high and surmounted by a spiral of barbed wire seems to go around it all and the portal is guarded by two dominant shapeshifters. Ashley gets out of the car without waiting for us and the brown guy runs towards her to hug her while making her spin in the air. I can't stop showing my fangs to this rival who touches my partner and i barely hold back my groan. Only Owen is not fooled and realizes my dissatisfaction. He frowns at me and beckons me to calm down. I join my partner, who has released her grip, and she presents this animorph to me that I already hate.

— Greg, this is Sean, the Guardian Angels beta, and Owen. Sean, Owen, this is my friend Greg, a Treat lieutenant.

— I have also been her personal bodyguard for years.

— And where were you yesterday?

My voice has nothing of human, it looks more like a cavernous growl. Ashley glares at me while Greg looks contrite.

— I'm sorry Ash. I should have been there to defend you, but we thought the threat was gone and you asked me to leave. Once I got there, you were gone.

— No worries Greg. Don't worry. You had no reason to stay with me. I was the one who didn't want you to stay. And Sean has no complaints about you.

She shows compassion and understanding in front of her friend and gently rubs his arm. I want to tear it away from him to make his smile disappear. Why can't i have the same consideration? Because I didn't give her any reason to have it. My heart sinks painfully at this observation. Whatever I do, I am certainly not up to what she expects from a man. Maybe because I'm not really one. The lieutenant's crisp voice brings me back to the present moment.

— Peter is waiting for you. It’s time he saw you

safe and sound, he was starting to lose his legendary self control and shout at everyone.

— Let's go right now. See you later Greg.

We take our vehicle and we plunge through the peaceful and wooded space. The area seems much larger than I expected. It takes us another quarter of an hour to reach a sort of huge hangar, lost among the trees, and highly secure in view of the guard on duty, the armored door and the keypad used to open the door.

— It looks like the Treat Alpha has things to hide.

— You don't want to shut it up, a little.

Ashley seems angry at me and that's not what I wanted at all. In all honesty, having a building like this necessarily hides secrets. The door opens on a man of impressive body, even for me. His face is frank and lights up with a dazzling smile at the sight of Ashley who hugs him. Again ??? She wants my death, or rather, that of other males, to rub against them like that. This visit will turn into a bloodbath at this rate. The aura of domination that emanates from this man makes me restrain my fulminating lion. This alpha, behind his nonchalant look, has an undeniable force and one would have to be crazy, or suicidal, to provoke him. I then notice his outfit: a doctor's coat. I am more and more intrigued.

— Ash, sweetie. Glad to see you're okay. But I feel you tense. Any problem ?

—Nope. I'm just still allergic to authority.

The so-called Peter then looks at us in turn with interest.

—I see. So your aversion is not limited to Nathan?

I feel my partner become nervous at the mention of this first name.

— Looks like no. It's for betas in general.

He laughs by hugging her. He will drop her at the end! My behavior does not escape him. Normal, my lion is literally fighting against me to go out and I am convinced that my eyes are its. Even my nails tend to get longer to be replaced by claws. He apparently does not take offense and distances himself from the one who will certainly drive me crazy soon, if it is not already done, without taking his eyes off me.

— There is a fine line between love and hate. You should think about it Ash.

Looks like I'm denounced. This alpha is a little too insightful for me. Owen's amazed reaction proves to me that he also understood the hint. Only my indomitable bride frowns without understanding.

— Hello. I'm Peter Browling. Excuse my outfit, I worked in the laboratory and I have not seen the time passed. It was better by the way. It seems that my bad mood was starting to scare away the members of my pack. You must be Sean and Owen from the Guardian Angels pack?

I bow my head as a sign of assent and respect.

— Your alpha, Connor, has notified me of your visit. I wanted to thank you for saving my girl mule head.

Only it is not his daughter and I do not appreciate that he is so close to her.

— Your adopted daughter, if I'm not mistaken.

— Exact. She is no less my daughter. Better than anyone, you know there is no need for blood ties to make a family.

I remain motionless for a moment. Would he know about me? Impossible, apart from the governor, nobody knows my story, not even the members of the pack. My distrustful and lost air makes him clarify his thoughts.

— Your pack is out of the ordinary. You are still a close—knit family.

—Effectively.

I relax slightly and get to the main problem.

— We would like your permission to take Ashley to our territory. Her friend Sevana wants to see her.

— And my permission doesn't count?

I close my eyes to the remark of my partner. If I don't hold back, my lion will bite her right away and show her who commands here. It would certainly not be a good idea. Peter realizes my inner turmoil and intervenes.

— Ashley, let me chat with our guests, please. You should take the opportunity to go see Sam.

His face begins to glow at the invocation of this first name and I take a new blow to my heart. Many people count for her in the Treat. Would she be ready to leave them for me? Certainly not immediately.

— Good idea. See you later.

I watch her run away without being able to do anything about it.

— Don't be so tortured. Ashley is a free spirit. You have to accept her like that. Since when do you know that she is your soul mate?

— Since we passed to her home, just before coming.

— Ah. Her smell is more concentrated in her apartment.

Owen is lost.

— Why didn't you say anything?

I erase his question from my head and try to solve part of the mystery.

— Why is her smell different on her, more evaporated and fickle?

— It's not up to me to tell you. Just know that she is an extraordinary person and that she deserves all the affection you already have for her, and more. However, she will not be easy to convince. She never goes out with shapeshifters although she knows a lot and some have not hidden their interest for her.

— Are you telling me that so that I can disembowel one of your members? Sam maybe?

It gives him a smile.

— Calm down, feline. Sam is not a threat to you. Not in that sense anyway. What animal are you?

Why would I surrender with no condition?

— You first.

— A leopard, like all members of the Treat.

—I am a lion.

— Well, then you don't risk anything. And now follow me, I've worked enough for today.

We walk side by side while Owen stands back, scanning the surroundings and tender our ears at the slightest noise. We enter a large house with male decoration. There are pictures there, only of Ashley and a young woman who looks a little like her, but redheaded and taller despite a youthful face. Ashley seems to be close, but the redhead seems elsewhere and sad. I didn't know she had a sister. One more obstacle to overcome to convince her to settle with me.

— These are my two daughters. I love and protect them, whatever it costs me. I will not let anyone approach them without making sure they are safe.

His remark almost sounds like a threat.

— I would never hurt Ashley.

— That goes without saying. You would regret it, otherwise. You would be wrong to underestimate her. Others made this mistake and regretted it bitterly. She is far from being a fragile flower and her sister, in short, do not make this mistake.

I never thought otherwise. She doesn't let herself be trodden on. Including by me.

The alpha settles into an armchair after serving three cups of coffee and invites us to do the same.

— Now explain to me why my daughter was attacked and why you took her with you instead of bringing her directly to her family.

Owen explains the situation, omitting certain information.

— The Black pack is looking for Sevana, Ashley's friend, and hopes to reach her thanks to your daughter.

— Human? What can they want to her?

I shake my head and Owen keeps his lips sealed. No way to talk about the fatels.

— Ashley never introduced her to me. She even did everything to avoid this moment. I guess this has a relationship?

Little smart. She protected her friend from her own pack.

— I take your silence for a yes. It seems that my treatment worked wonders on Miss Slat. I am very pleased.

What? What is he talking about ?

— Your treatment?

— I am the inventor of gene therapy based on metamorphic genes.

That's why the name of Peter Browling was not unknown to Liam. He was right.

— This is what allowed Sevana to heal at an accelerated speed. We owe you a lot, thank you.

— Every life is important, whether human or metamorphic. Was there no side effect?

— No. Connor only talked about her smell, which

was different.

I understand the significance of my words when I say them and Peter's knowing smile tells me that I have told something important.

— I make drugs for a lot of reasons. Not just for the sick.

I jump up.

— I need to see Ashley. I need to talk to her.

— Good. It's on your left as you go out. Straight on for twenty minutes. The first house on the right.

— Thank you.

I'm running like crazy. I think I guessed. Ashley hides her scent, her apartment smells of magic and she knows the fatel. I absolutely have to know if my hypothesis is the right one.

Chapter 10

Ashley

I go to Sam's house with enthusiasm. It’s been so long since I’ve seen her. Besides, I really needed to get away from Sean. He is so ... so too much ... everything. Too beautiful, too angry, too authoritarian, too sexy, too exciting. Damn, I'm completely lost in the face of what I feel in his presence. I feel like I am confused and my talent is useless. His lion prevents me from perceiving anything other than his rage. An intense and ancient rage, the origin of which I cannot capture, and which feeds on his least annoyance. Which is not lacking since nothing is enough to annoy him.

I knock on Sam's door and enter without waiting. I'm worried about the condition I'm going to find her, but Peter has assured me that she is doing well and that the treatment seems to be working.

— Sam, where are you?

— Ash?

My little sister runs towards me and jumps into my arms. I missed her so much. I promise myself that I will never stay so long without seeing her again. Almost a month without looking at her porcelain doll face is too much. She will be 30 next month, she is an adult, but I am aware that she still needs me. Her mind is traumatized and my presence, coupled with my power, allows her to stabilize. Peter has been trying to create a treatment that would have the same effect on her through my blood for years, but it turns out that it is more complex than that of animorphs. The task is therefore difficult and long. The last drug still seems to have positive effects. We must now wait to see in the long term. Sam has a shy smile and my power only captures a hint of gloom, but no morbid image and no terror. It's a good day for her.

— Ash, you stay in the pack for a long time?

I am sorry to have to disappoint her as soon as I arrive.

— No, Sam. I'm just passing. I have to go see my friend Sevana. I already told you about her.

She nods. She is the only person to whom I have confided that Sevana is special, although I did not tell her why.

— I could come with you. I'm fed up. Peter prevents me from leaving the territory. He treats me like a kid.

— I know Sam. It's for your own good. And I can't take you. Sevana is in another pack.

— I have better control, you know? come on please ?

My little sister is still, in many ways, a little girl.

— So why did I see Dany leaving and holding his nose?

She pouted and turned away from me, shunning my gaze.

— He was boring me.

I shake my head, annoyed.

— This is not a reason to make him bleed and you know it.

She folds in on herself and gloomily, I feel her sink into sadness.

— Will you come back soon?

This vision saddens me. I am living my life when my sister is stuck in the past and I can do nothing for her.

—Of course. As soon as possible. Nothing can ever keep me away from you, you know that.

We chat for a few more minutes, then I go to my house. Or rather, my old house. The house Peter gave me on the territory when I wanted to gain independence. Nothing has moved inside, each object is in its place. My father made sure that nobody touched my house, in case, I say, I want to return to my family.

I don't have time to rest that my door opens on Nathan. He was the last person I wanted to see and the surprise was more than unpleasant.

— Hi Ashley. Glad you came back. Can we talk ?

Talk ? No, certainly not. Each time, he broachs the same subject and I'm too tired to face this conversation tonight. I just want him out of my house.

— Another time Nathan. I'm tired.

— I can take care of you, you know. As a companion must do.

Here we go again. Always the same story. So it will never stop?

— I'm not your partner and you know it.

— Of course yes. It's the drugs that Peter makes you take that blocks your perception of the bond, but I feel it. Your smell attracts me. You are my soul mate. Just seal the link for you to know it.

Whatever. The drugs change my smell, not my feelings. And for him, I only feel disgust and annoyance. For another beta that I would not name, however ... In short, this is not the time to think about it. I could be excited and Nathan would probably misinterpret this phenomenon.

— That's enough Nathan. We are not soul mates and I ask you to leave my house.

His gaze suddenly becomes bad and his animal prevents me from seeing in him. My gut screams at me to leave, but he is the Treat beta and I am part of the pack. I can't imagine that he wants to hurt me despite his insistence to claim me.

— Don't forget that you forced me to.

He then throws himself on me, making me fall on the sofa, and pinches my arms above my head with an iron fist. He crushes me with all his weight while lying on me, blocking my breathing in my burning lungs. I can hardly speak.

— Stop it, I'm not yours. You're wrong. You will regret it when you realize it.

He sneers like a possessed.

— Obviously you are not my bride. You are not even of my race. But if you had accepted our union, the bite would have been pleasant.

He then plunges his canines into my neck, placing his free hand on my mouth to stifle my cries of suffering. I then feel the horror of Sevana's aggression and pray silently that my ordeal will end quickly. My wish comes true when someone knocks on the door, interrupting Nathan in his suction. The beta tightens his grip on me, taking my breath a little more.

— No sound my little darling. Or I swear I would last this moment as long as possible.

I move my head painfully to signify my agreement and at the same time try to deploy my power to give him a psychic blow. Unfortunately, I run into his leopard which shows me the fangs.

— Tss, tss, tss. What do you think you're doing there? You forget that I know you.

These words whispered in the hollow of my ear so intimately make me want to vomit.

— Ashley, I know you're here. Open me.

Sean. He knocks on the door with his fist. I didn't expect to be so happy to hear his voice one day.

— If you don't open the door, I'll break it down.

Always so friendly. I silently thank him for being so dictatorial. I'm sure he's not kidding and luckily for me Nathan is sure too. He licks the wound he inflicted on me and gives me one last warning before fleeing from behind.

— Don't try anything or your sister died.

It takes me a while to realize what just happened. A member of the pack, a leopard supposed to protect me, attacked me. He drank my blood. I jump when the door opens with a crash, coming out of its hinges under the violence.

Sean appears before me, very angry, but his face changes color when his gaze falls on me.

— Ashley?

He now seems worried and his voice turns white when his eyes rest on my neck.

— Who did this to you?

I sit up as best I can and Sean comes to my rescue helping me to sit down. I then stutter on him to tell Peter. He does so by taking me gently in his arms.

—You should have told me.

He adds nothing more and his caressing voice tells me that he is more worried than angry. We don't say another word until Peter arrives. The alpha goes home jokingly.

— The door teared off, it is not a bit exaggerated... ASH! What is this mess? You!

My alpha grabs him by the collar and Sean lets himself be done so as not to poison an already complex situation. I intervene before the leopard hits my savior.

— It's Nathan. Nathan attacked me.

Peter instantly loosens his fist and Sean returns to my side. His presence is comforting and reassuring. Surrounded by these two colossi, I know that nothing can happen to me. Peter is paralyzed and stares at me, blank stare.

— Can you repeat ?

— Nathan jumped on me and bit me.

I turn my head to the side so he can see the wound on my neck. These eyes squint and are replaced by those of his leopard while his body contorts. Peter fights against the metamorphosis that his animal wants to impose on him to go hunting. Only one thing can hold him back.

— You have to protect Sam. He threatened her.

Sean hugs me a little more and tenses his jaw, but I don't have time to worry about it yet.

— Peter. No one can approach her except us and Greg.

— OK. I go. Stay here. You don't risk anything anymore with Sean by your side.

The beta nods. Do they trust each other? I must have missed an important conversation.

— Nothing will ever happen to her again.

— Good. I entrust her to you. My lieutenants will find this traitor and he will be punished accordingly.

— I will join them. I need to move and make myself useful.

— Okay, Owen. I accept your help. Let's leave them alone. They have a lot to say.

For sure. The way Sean looks at me, he's waiting

for answers and my secret is probably out of date because of this bite. There are only two reasons why a shapeshifter drinks a person's blood. Either it is for the bond of union, to mark her, or it is for power. But for power, there has to be magic. And Sean knows it because he knows Sevana and the reasons for her assault by shapeshifters. In addition, the spark at the bottom of his pupil intrigues me. It looks like desire. Only, he's been so snappy until now. Error, until we stop at my apartment. What made him change his mind there?

Chapter 11

Sean

I can't believe it. A male from the Treat attacked my partner. He left a mark on her skin, where I'm supposed to mark her to make her mine. This observation is difficult to bear, but it also confirmed my suspicions. And feeling my partner cuddling in my arms with confidence warms my soul.

— You are a fatel.

No need to ask the question, I'm sure. But I want her to open up to me. I need to hear it from her mouth.

— Given the events, it's hard to hide it. Besides, you know about Sevana and she is doing very well. You accepted her as an alpha female.

Well, we're finally moving on. She is ready to be honest. It's up to me to stay calm so as not to rush her.

— Did you recognize the signs of her power in the hospital?

— Yes, from the first day. I didn't know a

prophetess had survived. But all her intuitions, as Sevana calls them, did not leave me doubting for long.

I caress her back up and down and feel her relax her muscles one after the other, melting a little more against me.

— Why didn't you ever tell her about it? You could have helped her.

Unintentionally, it still sounds like an accusation. Ashley must feel it that way too, because she is moving away from me.

— Sevana was wary of shapeshifters and I live among them. I protected her by being silent and keeping her away from this people.

I grab her hand and wrap my fingers around hers.

— I didn't mean that.

— It's a habit with you, i think.

I didn't steal it. However all is not lost, she leaves her hand in mine.

— Sevana didn't know what she was. She knows nothing about the fatels. She thought she was human.

My partner opens her eyes like saucers.

—Really ? I didn't realize it. I thought she was just keeping it a secret to protect herself. I could help her understand what she is and the extent of her powers.

I've already done it, but it’s lovely to propose it.

— Until how old did you live with your parents?

The mask of suffering that passes over her face pushes me to take her against me. Anyway, this is where she belongs. I would never let her go away again. But now is not the time to talk to her about this.

— until my 10th birthday. Until Peter took me with him.

— Did your parents entrust you to Treat when they understood the danger?

A tear rolls down her cheek.

—No. Peter saved us from a dissident pack that held my family prisoner.

— What?

I heard about it. The Fatels taken hostage by rebels. The trembling voice of my sweet twists my entrails and my lion rises to the surface, ready to intervene.

— The pack had captured us a few months earlier. With Sam, we were used as pressure mean so that our parents let themselves go and do nothing against the animorphs who came to drink their blood regularly. In exchange for their cooperation, the animorphs did not bite us.

She witnessed horror. I now understand why she is close to this Sam. They support each other as they should have done when they were children. But now I'm the one who would be there for her. I want to know her whole story to know her. This trauma had an impact on what she became and her vision on life. I wipe her tears from my thumb.

— Tell me the rest.

— The Treat were looking for a place to settle. You know the rules of shapeshifters, before settling on a territory, you must ask permission from the neighboring pack already installed.

I nod and patiently wait for her to resume, my eyes on her. The memories are still vivid in her mind.

— When Peter introduced himself to the alpha, he immediately felt the magic. And then he saw us, me and Sam, chained on the back of the room like trophies. He pretended to be interested in us in the same way as these monsters and approached me. At first I thought he was going to hurt me, but he just whispered in my ear. In reality, he wanted to know if there were other fatels prisoners. The alpha enemy did not let me answer and violently took him away from me by asking him to leave his territory. Of coursee he forbade them to stay in the area unless they wanted war and the Treat were forced to retreat.

— They had no chance to fight animorphs doped

with fatels blood.

— Yes. But I still gave Peter the info without anyone noticing. I knew he was our only hope. I had perceived his kindness and his will to save us.

I turn to her and guess her power.

— You're a telepath. You communicate by thought and read people's minds.

She turns her head towards me and looks at me intently.

— You know a lot about my people.

— I'll tell you my story later. Let's finish with yours first.

I already know she will go get the answers in my head if I refuse to give them to her. I could never hide anything from my soul mate. My lion will certainly not prevent her from entering my head. It will be an opportunity for it to rub against her and is just waiting for that. However, she accepts my request, for the moment. After leaning back on me again, she continues.

— The Treat came back furtively at night to free us. The rebels believed that they were invincible and were not wary of security. Only Sam had been taken to our parents, because she kept crying.

— Wait. Sam is a girl?

She shakes her head, a smile on the corner of her

lips.

— Sam is my little sister.

It is not possible. Was I jealous of her sister? The pretty redhead in the photos of the alpha house. Obviously. I'm even more of an idiot than I thought when it came to Ashley. Her face darkens when she resumes her speech.—

The Treat freed me, then they went to rescue my parents following my directions. Unfortunately, they arrived too late to save them. They only found their corpses, with Sam curled up by their side. She had witnessed the killing of our family and could not do anything. She was very young and her power was not yet what it is today.

— Did the rebels ever try to take you back?

— The Treat was looking for territory, so we moved a lot at first, to hide our tracks, and since neither I nor Sam had been bitten, the dissidents had no way of finding us.

— I'm sorry sweetie. Do you want to go see your sister? Make sure she's fine and the traitor hasn't touched her?

She shakes her head vigorously.

—Not at all. The murder of our parents traumatized her. She can't bear to see a bite on me. Besides, she hates Nathan. He's crazier than I think if he tries anything against her. She is a fearsome fatel, you can believe me.

This is annoying, because I intend to bite her. She is mine and I want to mark her to claim her. And I don't really want to be beaten or worse, let her sister reduce me to flesh. I know that certain fatels powers were impressive.

— Are you upset that my sister is unstable?

— No of course not. We all have our share of shade.

— So stop grunting.

Indeed, my lion manifests loudly. It wants to leave its mark on the one that is part of it.

— Sorry. I really want to leave my mark on you and that this is a problem for your sister does not enchant my beast and me.

She is adorable when she looks at me while tilting her head to the side.

—Why ?

— You must know, you are a telepath.

She is indignant at my answer.

— Who do you take me for? I don't spend my time invading people's thoughts. Everyone has the right to privacy.

And There you go. I still upset her. I see her getting up and pacing, more and more nervous.

— Really, you are an enigma. You look at me with envy, and few seconds after you attack me verbally . You were bossy and bitter until we got to my house. How does being a fatel change anything for you? Since you felt the magic in my apartment, you try to get closer to me. Do you want power too? Like Nathan?

I don't like the way she is thinking at all. I have a lot of faults, but I'm not hungry for power.

— You insult me there. I don't care about power. I'm beta for the Guardian Angels and I don't want to be alpha so don't compare me to a monster, you want. My place suits me very well, thank you. It’s not the magic that struck me about you, it’s your smell. It was neat in your apartment, but it's bland on you.

— Peter has developed a drug to blur my essence. This allows me to camouflage my origins. This allows me to live normally among people without having to look over my shoulder that I have not been spotted by an ill—intentioned animorph. I don't take it on weekends, when I'm not going out.

— At home, I was struck by the smell of cinnamon and lime. I'm addicted to this smell. I could never do without it even if my life depended on it.

I approach her like predators, peeking out, without arousing her escape instinct. She is absorbed in her reflection, no doubt trying to decipher my words. I hug her and she does not resist despite her distrust, allowing me to plunge my nose into her hair, as close as possible to her skull, where her smell is slightly transparent.

— What are you playing at ?

— I'm a beta. I never play.

— Obviously, I should have known.

— You feel the connection, don't you? You are my partner.

Her open mouth makes me want to nibble her lips, but I'm afraid she won't let me do it. My sweet has character. It is better if she does not want to be crushed by my dominant aura and my bad mood.

— If it were true, you wouldn't have rejected me like that. The companions attract each other, they do not repel each other.

— It is true. But what crossed my mind is difficult to explain. I'm not good at words and I don't want to speak badly again. Read my mind. Please.

— I can not. It's difficult on animorphs. It takes a lot of energy.

Not always, no. What makes exercise tiring is when the animal objects.

— Only if the animal refuses contact. My lion is calling you. He is looking forward to you.

— We will really have to discuss your knowledge of the fatel people you and me. You know more than I do. It's horrifying. I was far from having finished my apprenticeship when I lost my parents. Relax.

I can feel her intruding into my head and my lion welcomes her by roaring. It then rolls into a ball and lets her discover all that she has inspired us since our meeting: hope, disappointment, frustration, happiness and desire. An explosive cocktail of emotions that oppose each other. She does not try to discover my secrets and withdraws gently, after touching my beast that purrs with pleasure.

Chapter 12

Ashley

I can not believe it. I am his soul mate. I'm half of this devilish sexy beta. I have always secretly dreamed of being the destiny of a shapeshifter, they are passionate men with intense feelings who dedicate their lives to the happiness of their partner. There is no divorce among these people. But Sean? He seems so fickle and angry.

— I knew it as soon as I saw you, but your smell didn't match what I felt for you and that made me angry. I did not understand the intense attraction that I had for you, in total contradiction with my senses. I'm sorry sweetie.

I can see that. shapeshifters all hope to find their true soul mate. It must have been very frustrating to recognize it visually and to be fooled when approaching. It also explains my attraction to him despite his abhorrent behavior. I've been fantasizing about him since we met, while on the other hand, I wanted to slap him almost every time he opened his mouth. I'm not sure if I'm ready to handle his mood swings. I might as well be honest with him.

— I hate being given orders.

He is contrite and sheepish. The powerful beta is tiny in front of me and it's just adorable. Difficult to blame him.

— I promise to make an effort. Give me a chance to show you all the love I have for you.

How can you resist a statement like that? I'm willing to give him a chance, but I'm not ready to seal the link right away. First I need to make sure it can work between us.

I lift my head and dive into his gaze of molten gold where an immense desire for me shines. I feel myself melt against his muscular chest. I stand on tiptoe, holding his biceps swollen to keep my balance, and drop my mouth on his warm lips. One of his hands wraps around my hair and holds me by the neck to deepen our kiss. Our languages meet and begin a bewitching ballet, caressing and exploring in every corner.

— Your taste is as exhilarating as your smell, suave and sweet. I could never do without you, never.

I tenderly caress his raspy cheek, hoping not to shatter all his hopes. I would be blame myself if I hurt him, but I don't want to trick him.

— I want you Sean, really, but I'm not ready for you to claim me. We've only been arguing since we've known each other.

He doesn't even wink.

— I'll wait. I will prove myself and you will accept me as a companion. All I ask you is to stay with me.

I sigh, but can't avoid a ball of happiness burst in my chest.

— Authoritarian and stubborn. I'm lucky.

— Hey, I'm sexy too, it can be catched.

He's not wrong. He has a very attractive physique, the kind that you want to explore with your fingertips and your tongue for hours. The bump on the front of his zip tells me he would be ready. But reality takes over and calls to order.

— Hum hum. Excuse me for disturbing you two, but we have a problem.

Owen contemplates us and his serious tone instantly brings me back down to earth.

— Did you catch Nathan?

—Not really. Rather, he was the one who found us. He just challenged Peter.

What? So that was the bad intentions that I caught on the periphery of his mind. It was his plan from the start. He wanted to claim me to drink my blood and be strong enough to beat Peter and take his place. His ambition and his vanity are limitless.

Sean is very dark next to me. He must have come to the same conclusion. The problem is that an alpha is forced to take up the challenges against him if he wants to keep control of his pack and therefore his place. It's Sean who inquires afterwards. I'm too tormented for that.

— When will the fight take place?

— Early in the morning.

When my blood is most perennial in Nathan's body.

— Stay with Peter. Make sure that the traitor is not preparing one more bad blow to make sure of the victory.

— The alpha is with Sam. Who is this Sam by the way?

Hula. It is better that he don't go to her house.

— Sam is my younger sister. You have to avoid approaching her. Stay outside of her house. Do not enter under any circumstances. She is not really sociable.

Sean gestures to his lieutenant not to ask questions and I thank him in thought. He looks at me, amazed, and nods. I didn't do anything extraordinary. It's an innate power for me and his lion is very cooperative. It is so happy to make a place for me by its side.

— I'm going to do rounds around to make sure the

danger is out for now.

Once Owen is gone, Sean kisses my temple, holding my hand.

— Let's go to bed, you have to rest. You lost a lot of blood. I'm going to clean your wound and put you to bed.

Is he going to make me think he intends to sleep with me? It seems to me that shapeshifters are insatiable towards their partner. And he wants to make me believe that he only wants to sleep with me? A priori, he reads thoughts too . If I hadn't seen him as a lion, I might think he's a telepath like me.

— I just want to hold you against me tonight. Don't get me wrong, I'm dying to explore your body and make love to you. Only my lion is far from being docile and I could not prevent it from biting you if I touch you.

He has the merit of being honest. However, I would like to know why his lion is so uncontrollable. It’s quite unusual for shapeshifters. In general, man and beast form a whole in harmony. Not that I'm worried. A beast will never attack its half. But I’m curious to find out the reasons for the underlying rage that I’ve already felt.

— I will tell you about my past as you told me about yours, we promise. But later. For the moment, you need to take care of yourself and rest. I absolutely want to attend tomorrow's fight. This Nathan has to pay for what he did to you and if I can't punish him myself, I want to at least attend.

I cajole him, understanding his desire for revenge, and lead him into the bathroom. Now is not the time to snoop into your past . He is sufficiently annoyed by my attack.

— Hide your claws my kitten. Peter will make him pay.

At least, I hope so. My blood made Nathan stronger and Peter may be a strong alpha, he is not invincible. He is a great alpha, tough, but fair, and replacing him would be a tragic loss to the pack, not to mention the pain it would do to my heart. Sam would likely have a severe dementia attack and we would likely be used for our power. No, I'm getting carried away. Peter will not lose and Sean will defend me against all odds. And he would surely protect Sam too, if I asked him.

Once Sean has gently cleaned my bite and some grunts, obviously, he borders me and sticks to my back, in the position of the spoon. His arm around my waist, his hand caressing my belly next to the skin, gives rise to chills along my spine. I am so relaxed in his presence, wrapped in his warmth and musky smell of male, that I am asleep quickly, noting that there is a monster erection stuck against my buttocks.

All her muscles relax and her breath is regular, her rib cage goes up and down in a slow rhythm, attracting my gaze on her chest which I am dying to caress. I must be maso for having proposed to sleep with her, in her bed, without touching her. Her essence of cinnamon and lime is rising to the surface, she must not have taken her damn pill that blurs my senses, and puts me in torment. A carbine erection tries to punch a hole in my pants. After several hours of gentle torture, I can't stand it any more and get up before making an irreparable mistake that will put Ashley in a black anger. Any way, dawn is approaching. I need to contact Connor to update him on the latest changes, this will cool my libido. Our return to Guardian Angels territory will have to wait for the situation to stabilize, and I don't think Ashley will agreeto get separate from her little sister. We will therefore have to prepare for her arrival which, as I understand, will require some special precautions. A priori, it can be dangerous. My sweet will have to brief me on Sam's power so that we can adapt an appropriate environment to her.

— Connor, we can't go home right away.

— And why this ? It must be important for you to get me out of bed so early in the morning.

Shit. I didn't pay attention, but Connor doesn't have the same frustration concerns as I do. Although, now, that he had to let go of his partner to answer the phone.

— Ashley got bitten by the Treat beta.

— Did she bond with a shapeshifter?

I roar at this idea.

— Surely not. She's mine !

— Calm down Sean. It is early to wake up a whole pack with your screams. I do not understand.

— Ashley is my soul mate and a fatel, like Sevana. Beta drank her blood and challenged her alpha.

Silence settles down on the other side of the phone, until Connor understands the meaning of my words.

— She is much more in danger than expected. If this traitor wins, we risk having a new dissident pack on the arms. When will the fight take place?

— In few hours.

— Stay close to your partner. We come as reinforcements as quickly as possible.

Two alphas in one place is a bad idea in general, but Connor and Peter are more civilized than most. And then there's Sam's problem.

— Connor, Ashley has a sister. She is traumatized. I don't know how much, but as far as I understand, few people can approach her.

— Don't worry about it. Nothing will separate you from your other half. They will both be welcomed with open arms. You saw well with Sevana, the whole pack accepted her. Pay attention to yourself and protect them while waiting for us.

It relieves me that my pack comrades are coming in for reinforcement. While waiting for their arrival, I'm not going to leave my partner for a second, that's for sure.

Chapter 13

Ashley

The sun is barely on the horizon when Sean touches my cheek with the tips of his fingers, soft words puffed into my ear with the tip of his lips.

— Wake up pretty. You're beautiful lit by the first rays of the sun, a real goddess, but a great breakfast is waiting for you.

Um, I could quickly get used to this kind of wake up every morning. Only one thing is missing ... oh no, there it is. The tender kiss that teases me and electrifies my whole body. I run my hand behind his neck and brings him closer to me, crossing the barrier of his teeth with my tongue to taste it.

— I'm a hundred percent on the same wavelength sweetie, but we don't have time and I'm not going to be able to hold back long from taking you if you continue like this.

What is he saying? We always have time for a hug with a man with a dream body. The mist in my brain is slowly evaporating and the reality of the situation is hitting me hard. We don't have time. Unfortunately. For once, I'm the one who growls in frustration.

— I forgot for a moment.

I sit up in bed and open my eyelids on a very excited Sean with those burning eyes and the bump in his jeans. In fact, it seems to be in the same condition as yesterday when I fell asleep.

— Sorry. I didn't mean to warm you for nothing.

—No problem. I've been in this state since I first smelled your perfume. It's not going to pass.

Oops. I lick my lips with envy and make her groan.

— I promise to solve your problem (I point his jeans zip with my index finger) as soon as possible.

A mischievous smile lights up his face.

— I should hope so my sweetie. I will remind you of your promise as soon as the opportunity arises.

I'm eating the delicious meal that Sean made for me and I'm going to change without wasting a second. I would have liked to have seen Sam before going to see Peter, but the bite is still very visible on my skin, I am not a shapeshifter, I do not heal at high speed like them. I don't want to worry her unnecessarily. Greg will stay with her during the fight. I have full confidence in him. I'm more worried about Peter and Sean. I wish I could help

Peter, but Nathan's animal is strong and won't let me enter his mind. I do not know if his intentions are limited to taking power or if it is only the beginning. As for Sean, luckily his lion is cooperative. This will allow me to calm him down, because I don't think he will know how to control himself in the presence of my attacker.

— Ashley, you have to go if you want to see Peter before the confrontation.

— Okay. Sean, I have a request before we leave. Keep your cool over there. Whatever happens.

He is already growling, slightly rolling up his lips. I realize this is his way of communicating. I'm just going to have to get used to his cranky side.

— This traitor attacked you, he spilled your blood, and you ask me to do nothing and say nothing?

— I know, it's difficult for you. But Peter will avenge me. Itis his alpha duty and I can assure you that he will be ruthless. I'm his daughter, remember?

— Okay, for you. But swear to me that you will stay close to me all the time. Don't go away at any time.

He looks so tortured. His protective instinct fights with his feelings.

— I promise you, I'll stick to you like a leech.

Peter's house is in sight far too quickly for me. The whole pack is there and I am relieved to see that they have all, without exception, come to support Peter. Whatever Nathan has in mind, whether he wins or loses, the pack will never accept him as an alpha. All show me the respect as the chef's daughter even if i am not, however. Not really. They have always considered me as such, however, and they have accepted Sam as she is, without ever blaming her for her deviations which cause them annoyance each time. I realize today how lucky I am to have come across them. I love them as much as they are.

— Ashley, come here.

—Peter. Pay attention to yourself.

Why is he so confident? The pack is behind him, but has no right to intervene during the duel.

— Don't worry about me. Everything will be alright. Stay with your companion no matter what.

Definitely, if I did not understand that I must stay with Sean, it is that I am an idiot. But ?

— You knew ?

— Of course. Don't tell me you didn't notice the way he looks at you and growls every time a man approaches you.

Very funny

.— He growls all the time!

Sean nibbles on my earlobe while Peter laughs.

— He's a dominant lion. You'll get used to it. And then, you have the ideal character to support him. It's time. Do what I told you. Obey for once.

I stand in anguish with my pack brothers, Sean behind my back, on the lookout. Nathan enters the circle formed by the Treat with his head held high, under their snapping teeth. A pack of raging leopards now surrounds the two protagonists. Nathan is visibly surprised by their welcome, he looks at them, annoyed.

— Stop your cinema. Peter is weak. He welcomed a fatel into our midst as one of ours instead of using her to conquer territories. I will make the Treat unforgettable and invincible.

I hold Sean in extremis before he leaps forward and the Treat find it difficult to not to do the same.

— Hush, baby. Calm down.

He kisses the top of my head, obviously very pleased with the nickname I gave him. This lion is easier to coax than I thought, even if its rage continues to boil inside.

— No more bla bla Nathan. You wanted a challenge. Here I am in front of you.

Peter transforms into a leopard in a micro second.

This phenomenon has always impressed me. In place of the alpha is a majestic beast of fawn color abundantly spotted in black, all in finesse despite well—developed muscles. Nathan get transformed too. His leopard is smaller, more stocky, less impressive, and his aura of domination is ridiculous beside the power released by the alpha. He immediately jumps on our chef who dodges at the last moment. A little too late to be able to avoid a bite on his back leg. The wound is not deep, but bleeds profusely, staining the ground under the alpha. Confident about his victory, Nathan is gaining momentum to notch his opponent's blank with a blow of sharp claws. Peter shifts again at the last moment, not being able to avoid, once again, the touch of a fingernail on his coat.

— What is Peter playing at?

Sean's breath in the hollow of my neck and tickles me, but I stay focused on the fight. His interrogation still joins mine. I’ve already seen Peter fight. His leopard is fierce and gets straight to the point. There, it looks like he's just having fun. Is he afraid? Is he waiting for Nathan to get tired? The beta, sure of his blow, tries to jump on the back of Peter who lies on his back and projects the traitor in the distance thanks to a powerful extension of his 4 legs. The leopard flies through the air and crashes hard on the ground. All felines do not fall on their feet it seems. The alpha turns peacefully around his prey, without hurrying. Sean is right. My father has had fun from the start. He has not shown what he is capable of. The smallest leopard tries to grab his neck when Peter passes by, but only inherits an ugly cut on the nose. The rumblings become more powerful, Nathan chattering teeth, the fangs uncovered, while Peter continues his nonchalant round, wagging his curved tail raising the dust. Nathan, contrary to the appearances that their respective injuries suggest, loses control of the situation and tries desperately to strike the alpha who jumps and bounces, seeming to be greatly amused by the disappointment of his opponent. Events follow when the beta directs his rage against me when he approaches. Sean reacts to the quarter turn by placing himself in front of me, but does not have time to sketch slightest attack as Peter grabs Nathan's hind leg, yanking him away from me. He does not release him, on the contrary, accentuating the pressure of his jaw on the body part which cracks in a sinister noise. A howl of pain comes out of the traitor's feline throat, but that doesn't stop Peter, visibly running out of patience. He releases his paw to wickedly open the fur from eye to jaw, piercing his stomach with his rear claws in the same movement. Without giving him one more look, he turns away from him, exposing his back to him, notifying by his posture how little he cares about him, and resumes human form.

— You are nothing. You pose no threat to me or my

pack. You are weak and insignificant. You're far from having the makings of an alpha.

Nathan returns on his two legs and I see that one of them forms a strange angle. As for his cheek, the cut is deeper than his fur suggested. The beta holds his abdomen awkwardly trying to get up, with blood flowing profusely between his fingers.

— How ? You've created a formula that makes you stronger, admit it. You're just an imposter, an alpha with no legitimacy.

Peter laughs out loud. A disturbing and bad sneer that gives me chills.

—No. I don't have to cheat to beat a woodlouse like you. Even a child could beat you up. Do you think you are strong? In reality, you are pathetic.

He snaps his fingers and the lieutenants raise the traiteur under the armpits.

— Get him out of the territory. You are banished from the pack. One last advice before you leave, never attack a member of the Treat again or your punishment will be death without warning.

Sean is unhappy with the alpha decision, I can fell it. His body is rigid against me while Nathan is dragged outside. He wanted the extermination of the man who attacked me.

Peter joins us, mopping the few superficial scratches that ooze slightly, with a towel.

— He knows about Ashley. He knows her secret and has no sense of honor. Releasing him puts her in danger. You should have killed him to keep him from speaking!

I caress the roaring chest of my darling to soothe his torments and my spirit caresses his lion to comfort him. The few images I capture while consoling his beast are disturbing, even for me. People, men, women and children, on the ground, dead, bathing in a pool of blood. Terrifying memories that could come from Sam's tortured mind. There are so many people slaughtered, and I can feel my companion's pain, rage, helplessness and worry. He's afraid the same thing will happen to me. I don't know exactly what he went through, but I understand his permanent anger better. Who wouldn't be in his place. He has seen abominable things. We need to have a serious conversation as soon as possible so that I can understand him.

Peter lets out his alpha aura to keep Sean from hunting.

— Calm down lion. He won't say anything. He is a loner now, an easy prey. And if he talks about the fatel, he will have to explain why he lost the fight. It will not stick with his story.

Exactly. I would like to understand why he got beaten so easily. Normally, the alpha's victory was obvious, Peter is a fearsome leopard, but by swallowing my blood, Nathan should have grown in strength and been much stronger.

— You think too much my daughter. I see your neurons overheated from here. These are the tablets you are taking that have countered the effects of your blood. By changing your smell, it also changes your blood composition. This negates the effect it has on shapeshifters.

So that !!! I did not expect that.

— You knew it ?

— Of course. I designed it that way.

Sean smiles from ear to ear and looks at Peter with respect.

— You ensured her protection against all shapeshifters, including yours, by leave them in ignorance. You made sure no one could use her.

— That's it. There was a strong temptation for a greedy animorph to take advantage of the situation. I made it impossible. I told you, Ashley is my daughter and no one should ever hurt her. Not even you.

A lieutenant runs towards us.

— Alpha, Guardian Angels members are at the gate.

Peter nods while Sean doesn't seem surprised.

— Reinforcements, I guess?

— They wanted to come when I informed them of the betrayal in your pack. They said that a helping hand would not be luxury. In addition, there are things we need to discuss.

— Okay, let them in. Ashley, you should come see your sister.

Ask Greg to join me.

I am not allowed to listen? My father continues to keep me away from clan politics as if I were a little girl. No problem, my lion will tell me everything I need to know. There are no secrets between us, mainly because I am a powerful telepath who can get info from him if he does not cooperate, who does not seem ready to happen. His beast adores me. I kiss my man and go to my house. I have to cover up my wound before I find Sam or she's going to freak out. But there has been enough blood that has flowed for today.

Chapter 14

Dean

My revenge is approaching, I can feel it. This stupid Alice warned us that the Guardians were still prowling around and were taking a close interest in this nurse, Ashley Peterson. Unfortunately, my two lieutenants died and the third was unable to tell me why he was sprawled on the ground. I am surrounded only by incompetent people. I'm the Alpha of the Blacks, the most powerful pack of shapeshifters on this planet, but with so many losses in a short time, the clan is losing confidence in me and it is high time to fix it. I have to get hold of the hospital fatel. I will have to do everything myself if I want to keep control of the pack. Fortunately, the receptionist said everything she knew about the nurse before draining her blood. Humans are so fragile. Simple insects on my way that I crush.

Things seem to be moving in front of the Treat portal. It's a bad surprise that human are among the shapeshifters, but it's only a downside. She cannot remain hidden forever. The Treat are throwing an injured man out. This is interesting. And that could be very useful to me. shapeshifters are spiteful. Well, well. The Guardians are all here. And ... the woman in the car ... no, it would be too good! The hospital fatel? She looks like the description my beta gave me, before dying with the best dominants in the pack. The massacre that put my alpha position on the hot seat. Events finally turn to perfection, it seems. Luck smiles on me.

The exiled strolls away while the Treat escorts the new arrivals inside. No one in sight? So it's up to me to play.

— Need a halp?

— I don't need anyone.

A proud and belligerent animorph, my favorites. Who knows, once he gets back on his feet, he could be a good recruit. Once he will be subdued. We don't lack of respect for his alpha, unless he wants to die, of course.

— You owe me respect, brat.

— And on whom do I have the great honor of pissing the blood?

— Dean. I'm the alpha of the Blacks.

I see that my pack says something to him. His face suddenly lights up.

— Are you looking for someone?

A profiteer, in addition to the rest. The perfect candidate to help me.

— You know that perfectly. I need Ashley Peterson.

— Why ?

— Does she matter to you?

It would compromise my plans. I want a helping hand to catch her.

— Oh no! I have an account to settle with this bitch.

Perfect. We will get along well with him and me.

— I am going tu use her as bargaining . I'll deliver her to you as soon as I get what I want.

— It's a deal!.

I went around the territory as advised by the shapeshifter who turns out to be the beta of Treat. He doesn't have the power apparently. Following his directions, I find myself in the opposite of the gate, under the cover of the trees, in front of a hole in the fence hidden by ivy. Nathan disliked reporting on his whereabouts and set up a personal outing. The passage is narrow and I leave a few pieces of skin there, but I am inside the territory of Treat, far from the house of the alpha. And according to my new ally, very close to my target. I sit in the shade of a house, out of sight, but with the building that interests me in sight. I do not wait long before I see the nurse disembarked, a smile on her lips. I will make the joy of her face disappear. I jump in front of her, making her jump, surround her neck and press a few seconds on these cervicals, cutting her nervous system. The hardest thing for me is not to kill directly, I'm not used to restraining myself. She quickly falls into my arms like a rag doll. Humans are unable to defend themselves. I am surprised by the sound of a door slamming nearby. Better not to linger. I quickly throw the woman on my shoulder and make the opposite way to discreetly leave the territory of Treat. Child's play even with my package. And to say that three of my men failed to do this in a hospital parking lot. I am surrounded by incompetent people.

The hideout I found is only an hour's drive from the fatel position, but it is discreet and well hidden. In addition, the car journey seemed much longer with Nathan complaining and moaning all the time. I end up believing that he's not as smart as he looks. And much less beefy. These wounds begin to heal, but he continues to blow and whine. A real wimp. He's going to have to prove to me that he has guts or I'll leave him there.

I am very pleased to see the members of my pack. I would never admit to them, but they missed me and Sevana could certainly have advised me about Ashley, avoiding me making so many mistakes.

Connor and Liam came as backup. And Sevana. I can't believe she's here. She had to fight severely with Connor to let her leave the territory and go to unknown shapeshifters. And given the grunts he emits and his bad look, he is very unhappy.

— Do all your males constantly growl in your pack? Leopards are more measured.

Indeed, one could believe it.

— Peter, this is Connor, my alpha, his partner Sevana and one of our lieutenants, Liam.

—Nice to meet you. Sevana, like Ashley's colleague at the hospital?Connor pulls his soul mate back when she wants to shake Peter's hand.

— Recent union, I presume.

I don't think the problem is there. And since my alphas have been watching each other for a while, I guess Sevana is scolding him by telepathy.

— I said no, my angel.

— You stop or I hang you on top of a tree.

Our alpha female is not kidding and I hide my sneer behind a fake cough, like Liam and Owen. Peter's eyes go back and forth between the two protagonists and he also seems to be having a lot of fun. Of course, the fatel has the last word. It's because she has character. What do you want to do against someone who can hang you by the feet with a snap of fingers?

— Hello Peter. I'm actually Ash's friend.

I can see the alpha's eyes widening as she approaches him. We can't miss the smell of magic flowing through her veins.

— Ashley has kept your secret well. I understand better why she prevented our meeting, the little clever one.

— Actually, I didn't know everything about my origins, unlike your daughter.

— She's a powerful telepath, hard to hide anything from her.

Yeah, sure. My beautiful companion has a sharp mind.

Greg trots along, pinching his nose between his thumb and forefinger, dried blood under his nostrils, and chats with Peter.

— Sam made her own again?

The lieutenant shrugged casually.

— She didn't want me to be there anymore and I tried to insist.

—I see.

And me, I think that it will indeed be necessary to arrange her a space away from the pack. She seems to enjoy the loneliness and I don't want her to hit the Guardian Angels because they will annoy her.

— Did the fight go as planned?

— Yes. Ashley didn't tell you?

— I have not seen her.

Sorry ? She went to see her sister for a while. They must have crossed paths. Sevana then grabs my arm and her heartbeat accelerates. This does not bode well. My lion begins to turn in circle in my head, the lips quivering.

— Tell me.

—She is not there anymore.

My lion roars while Peter wants to know what's going on.

— Ashley has been kidnapped.

— GO AROUND THE TERRITORY. FIND ASHLEY.

The Treat's run off on the orders of their alpha, but I'm under no illusions. Sevana is never wrong. If she says my partner is no longer there, it is. Peter looks more closely at Sevana.

— A prophetess?

— Yes. We have to talk.

Chapter 15

Ashley

My last wake up was much better than this one. I am lying on the floor in a very uncomfortable position, my arms tied behind my back and my feet tied together. I try to collect my memories to reconstruct the events that led me here, but everything is a little confused. I remember the fight of Peter, the exile of Nathan and the announcement of the arrival of Guardian Angels. Then I went to Sam's house and ... I never got there. A man came out of nowhere and made me pass out.

— The little darling is finally awake. Wonderfull.

The man in front of me is unknown to me. He must be the age of Peter, in his sixties, and his eyes are cold, devoid of all expressions. A shapeshifter, undeniably. Very large, at least 1 meter 90, a very developed musculature, he releases a very powerful malicious aura.

— Where am I ?

— I'm the one asking the questions here. I'm the

Alpha of the Blacks, Dean.

I can't prevent my body shudder at that mention. I know what this pack is capable of. My reaction does not escape him.

— Perfect, I see that my reputation precedes me. So you know it's better for you to cooperate.

I keep my mouth shut and try a psychic attack that has absolutely no effect. His mind is hermetic to magic. It must have taken a lot of training to achieve this result. I am far from being the first fatel that crosses his path and this observation is far from rejoicing. Luckily, his wolf didn't spot me. However, another noticed my attempt.

— No foolishness Ash. Do nothing you might regret.

Nathan. He didn't just betray his alpha. I pinch my lips until I make a hard line to remember the names of birds he inspires me.

— You're going to call Peter Browling and tell him I'm ready to trade you for Sevana Slat.

Exchanging me ? That he wants Sevana is not a secret, but having another fatel does not interesst him? He didn't feel it and Nathan didn't say anything. So I'm in relative safety, he doesn't want to use me until death ensues. I would not suffer the same fate as my parents. But am I ready to sacrifice my friend to save my life? I don't even have to think about it to know that I don’t.

— I would never help you capture her. Rather die.

Saying to myself, I think about Sean, about his love for me and me more, because I love him, it is obvious, even if he annoys me sometimes, often even, he is anchored in my heart. I'm glad we didn't seal our link, because he wouldn't have survived my loss. United soul mates cannot live without one another.

— Don't do illusions Ash, you won't die. I have other plans for you.

Nathan's gaze slides over me and fills me with disgust.

— Don't do your innocent. I saw you rub the Guardian beta like a bitch in heat. You disappointed me a lot. Only you will be mine, forever.

There is worse than death. Being the companion of this traitor will be torture at all times. The alpha comes between us.

— I thought she didn't matter to you.

— And that's the case. Only I have revenge to take on her and her father and that it is a wonderful punishment to tie her to me. She can neither leave nor kill me, and her father will be forced to accept me as his successor.

They giggle together, their minds as twisted as each

other.

— I like your way of thinking. Call your alpha and if necessary, make him hear her screams. I don't want him to discuss my orders. Then she will be yours.

Sean

My partner was kidnapped. Who and why? It does not mean anything. She should have been safe on her territory. All of the Treat seemed to support their alpha. To hurt Ashley is to betray him. Greg comes to us for the second time today, his nose bloody. I take the lead while Peter does not react.

— Did you come across the kidnapper?

—Nope. I went to see Sam. It's nothing.

He sponges his nose while the alpha shakes his head from left to right, annoyed.

— We will have to adjust the treatment again.

I do not understand what treatment he is talking about and for now, I don't care. I want to find Ashley. Greg explains that he found a breach in the fence behind Sam's home, so he wanted to verify that she was well. Obviously, it is.

— Sevana, what do you see?

— Be patient. Everything gonna be alright.

The prophetess seems calmer than before, confident. It's very strange, but it helps my lion to calm down.

Suddenly, the alpha's cellphone rings and his face turns red.

— How dare you call me?

—…

— I'm putting on the speaker.

This call therefore concerns us. I recognize the voice from the first word.

— I have Ashley.

Beta traitor of the Treat. I'm going to dismember him before I disembowel him slowly. He's going to suffer before he gives up. I knew he shouldn't leave here alive.

— My colleague wishes to exchange. Ashley versus Sevana.

Connor tenses up by my side and responds tit for tat.

— No.

I can't even blame him for refusing. In his place, I would do the same.

— Where and when ?

Sevana’s questions surprise everyone and my alpha growls at her beloved. I'm sure there is a silent conversation going on between them, but the intervention of a new caller interrupts their mental communication.

— The fatel is courageous. I appreciate this quality.

— To whom have I the honor ?

— My name is Dean. We're going to spend time together you and me.

Connor screams in anger at the name. I have rarely seen him so pissed off.

— You are responsible for the death of my parents.

— Hahaha. I don't know what you're talking about. Who are you ?

— You are the alpha who ordered the attack on the Savage pack, twenty—five years ago.

The Alpha of Black is with my partner. The person who instigated the revolt and the massacre of the fatel. My grunts match those of Connor.

— The traitors who hid the fatels deserved death. I did proof of leniency in sparing young shapeshifters. I never thought I would be blamed for it one day.

Sevana takes her soul mate in her arms and comforts him with caresses on the face before continuing, imperturbable, plunging her gaze into that of her companion.

—Where and when ?

— Less grunts, gentlemen. We are civilized.

I refrain from breaking the phone in half and my lion lowers the sound level, just like the cheetah by my side.

— It's better. On the vacant lot close to the industrial zone west of the Treat territory. Come alone or your friend will die in horrible suffering. It seems to me that you know what we can do. Get under way right now, prophetess, or your friend is dead.

We hear Ashley's screams as the communication goes down. I can't stop my lion from taking control and find myself on all fours, roaring like crazy. Owen and Liam get on either side of my beast and Connor tries to force me to calm down using his alpha aura. However, what ends my bloodshed is the velvety voice of Sevana in my head. "Everything is fine, I have a plan. I'm going to bring you your partner unharmed . "I have full confidence in my alpha female and I sit on my hairy posterior to listen to her attentively, like all those around us.

— I'll go alone, as requested. I don't risk anything. He expects to see a helpless prophetess. He will take no precautions except to watch the surroundings.

She's right. Only, she is no longer a simple prophetess. I love the devilish smile that borders her lips. She is far from the fragile flower that she seems to be at first.

— Give me five minutes before you approach . I'll leave them to you.

Connor and I look at each other and make a carnivorous smile. Peter is completely lost, as is Greg.

— You are a prophetess. You are vulnerable to beta and alpha. What makes you so confident?

She gives him a dazzling smile.

— I'm less fragile than I seem. The union between a fatel and a shapeshifter has interesting repercussions on my people. Let us act. We will bring Ash back in no time.

The Treat Alpha nods despite his puzzled expression.

— Bring me back my daughter. That's all that matters to me.

My alpha couple and I set off without further delay, Sevana having assured us that everything would be fine this way. She didn't tell us about her vision, but if she is confident, so are we. And then, she didn't put us away. We also have our role to play. It will be a two-step attack and I would be ruthless. I'm sure Connor thinks the same as I do.

Chapitre 16

Ashley

— Why bring her if you plan to honor our deal and give her to me?

— The girl is a prophetess. She will know in advance if the hostage is absent and she will not come. Her presence is therefore essential. But do not worry. I do not intend to release her. I will honor our deal, the human is yours.

So that's why I'm tied up in the back of their car. I can't believe Sevana agreed to surrender. And even less than Connor lets her do. They certainly have a plan. I just hope no one will put themselves in danger for me. Nathan lifts me under my arms to get me out of the car while licking my neck. He has had fun clearing his throat with his teeth since he made the call. It made me scream the first time, I thought he was going to bite me again. Now, I just find it repulsive and hope to tear his tongue out as soon as the opportunity arises. If at least I could make him believe it, I would be very pleased.

I see Sevana walking slowly towards us, alone and

not at all intimidated. Where did the girl who hid as soon as a shapeshifter was near? She is not going to jump into the lion's den anyway! She looks at me intently and suddenly I hear her in my head.

— Are you ok Ash? Didn't they hurt you?

What ? How does she do it? She predicts the future, she is not a telepath!

— Do you hear me ?

— Yes but how…

— I'll explain to you later. Whatever happens, don't be afraid.

I was never afraid of her, why would it be different today? At the same time, I've never seen her wave her hands in front of her like she does now. I was so engrossed in gazing at her, intrigued, that I didn't see Nathan missing by my side until I heard him scream three meters away. And I certainly didn't expect the vision before me. The two shapeshifters are suspended in the air, literally, held two meters from the ground by an invisible force. They may struggle and contort in every way, they seem helpless. Suddenly, I feel a presence by my side and teeth nibble on the rope that binds my hands and feet. I stroke Sean's soft fur with my fingertips and he takes the opportunity to feel me and lick my neck, when purring. I frankly prefer this raspy tongue to that of the other pervert.

— Hi my dear.

Meanwhile, a beautiful cheetah rubs its head on the belly of my friend who always has her hands in the air and her gaze fixed on our enemies.

— They're yours, boys.

The blackmailers find themselves violently thrown to the ground in a sharp noise while Sevana staggers on her legs for a few steps and ends up sitting on the ground, visibly exhausted.

Sean immediately pounces on Nathan and grabs him by the throat without giving him the opportunity to transform. Anyway, groggy as he is because of the shock, he probably wouldn't have succeeded in taking his leopard shape. Which suggests to me that I too can get revenge. I enter his mind without difficulty, his beast having been struck by the fall as I supposed, and instills in him the nightmare he deserves. My mind weaves him a web in his consciousness like a spider, making him believe that I am tearing his tongue out with pliers and making him feel the pain associated with this torture. He passed out when Sean finished gutting him from the glottis to the navel.

Further on, the cheetah also quenches its revenge against the one who wanted to harm his companion, ripping the throat of the Alpha of the Blacks without an ounce of hesitation. I run to join Sevana whose eyes flutter with fatigue.

— You hid some of your talents from me, it seems. How can you have more power elsewhere?

She does not answer me and her head dangerously wobbles on her shoulders.

—Are you okay ?

She yawns and fights against sleep.

— The bond of union did miracles.

She has no time to clarify her thought that she falls into the arms of a very naked Connor, asleep.

— Come here my beautiful.

Sean wedges me against him and I find myself with my head buried against his chest.

— I'm the only one you have the right to see naked. Me and me alone.

— Okay. But there, you smother me.

He loosens his grip, but it is only to better take my breath away with a devastating kiss.

— Let's go to the Treat. My partner needs to rest.

Sevana is indeed inert in the arms of the alpha who holds her carefully.

Back at the Treat's and after a short visit to Peter, I'm finally home with Sean. I have nothing, except a few bruises where the rope damaged my skin and yet I feel him agitated. I wanted to rub his lion, but he was too angry to let me get into his head, I ran into a wall of rage. I want to know why. So I snuggle up against him on my bed, caress his chest, and question him.

— What's bothering you?

— The fact that you are a fatel and that you could have died like my family rekindles my rage against the rebel packs.

— I do not understand.

He kisses the tip of my nose, his eyes dark.

— I'm an orphan, like you. The only difference is that I am twice.

How can you be an orphan twice? I frown, but don't stop him. I'm just waiting for him to feel ready to continue.

— My biological parents, shapeshifters, died, one in a fight, and the other because of the break in the bond.

He pauses and I remain silent, giving him time to gather his ideas. I know the worst is yet to come, because it doesn't match the images I saw in his head.

— When my mother felt death approaching, she was near a traveling fatel camp . She explained the situation to them and asked them to find me a new family. They immediately agreed and continued on their way with one more passenger on board. I was just six months old. So I have no memories of my shapeshifters parents.

I feel sorry for him and hug him a little harder. My parents may have passed away, but I am fortunate to have memories of happy moments with them.

— The journey of the fatels lasted another six months, and during that time, the infant I was attached to them, and vice versa. So they decided to be the family I needed and I stayed with them.

He lived among the fatels. That's why he knows so much about my people. I'm afraid to hear the rest though. I know the end of the fatels.

— They taught me to be a good citizen while making me discover my lion nature and the difference between shapeshifters, fatels and human. They taught me that each of the peoples had their strengths and weaknesses, but that all of them had their uses.

It is true that the fatels were selfless and diplomats at heart. This is probably what caused their loss. They did not want to believe in the evil that prowled among the animorphs.

— One day, in my tenth year, my family asked me to make a retreat in a cave. They told me that it was an obligatory rite for shapeshifters lions and that a man would pick me up later, a human. They took me several kilometers from the house and I followed their advice, I slept for a long time.

I cry in silence as I guess what will happen next. They removed him to save him from the death that awaited them.

— A human actually picked me up the next day, but he refused to drive me home. I transformed and I ran to join my family, for distracting him. But there was no family.

His rage is palpable and I don't need him to describe to me the scene that has been torturing his soul for so long, I have already seen it. I prefer to direct the conversation towards a less painful subject.

— Who was the man?

He relaxes at this question, as I had hoped.

— Our current governor. I am the one who inspired his vocation. I was in the orphans home and he made sure that I was wanting for nothing. When he told me about the Guardian Angels project, a pack of shapeshifters who would fight injustice, I told him that I would be part of it. He agreed, but on one condition. Let me form a duet with a more diplomatic person because I was too angry to lead this project alone. So he hired Connor to team up. Over time, the pack formed and I became the beta.

He caresses my hair, looks sad, and his lion cries in

my head.

— Your fatel nature worries me, because the dissidents are still alive and you are a target for them. I'm afraid that I can't protect you. I love you too much to accept your loss.

— I understand. But your lion is powerful. I don't risk anything with you.

I'm trying to lighten the mood with a little humor.

— And our bond will perhaps give me super cool powers like those of Sevana. Then I could kick your butt or hang you from the ceiling when you give me an order.

On the way back to the Treat, Connor and Sean enlighten me on Sevana's sudden abilities. Like them, I was unaware that this phenomenon existed and I admit that I still find it hard to believe.

— Will you seal the link?

— I love you Sean. I want to stay by your side forever. But be prepared for the fact that I will spend my time ignoring your orders and constantly disobeying you.

— And I'll spend my time punishing you.

He kisses me just under the ear then descends along my collarbone to come and kiss the top of my chest. My nipples stand up and he grabs one end between his teeth, tickling his tongue before moving on to the second. If my punishments look like this every time, I want to be punished every day, and even several times a day, even if i provoke him just for that. Sean excites my senses and my passion with his teeth and his tongue, torturing me and creating a painful void in me that I want him to fill as quickly as possible. When he finally penetrates me, I literally lose ground. He borders on all of my nerve endings in an exquisite way. I am nothing but sensations and do not delay enjoying in a cry of ecstasy. He chooses this moment to bite me in the crook of the neck, linking our destinies, and spills into me an instant later. The feeling in my head is extraordinary and his lion is more than satisfied, purring and rubbing against my mind.

Epilogue

Ashley

— It's time to go home to the Guardian Angels. I am the beta and I have been absent for far too long.

— I already told you that I would not leave without my sister.

We have the same conversation for two days. Only today Sevana is in great shape and the Guardians are ready to return to their territory.

— You know very well that she is unstable. She can be dangerous. She needs to stay here with Peter.

— So I stay with the Treat with her.

— Stop being so stubborn. You are my partner, you stay with me and my place is with the Guardians.

He gets on my nerves when he wants to decide everything. I am so angry that I feel my blood boiling in my veins. I would never give up on my sister, and so Greg, who decided to go wherever she goes (I suspect he's got a crush on her), even if I understand my companion's reluctance.

— Ashley, you should calm down.

— Don't tell me what to do.

— Sweetie, you're igniting.

— No, I'm not igniting, as you say. I just want you to understand that ...

— Baby, your hands.

— What are my hands?

Sean steps back as I raise my hands before my eyes and I see sparks at my fingertips.

— SHIT! Sean, help me!

He rushes to take me in his arms and cradles me tenderly.

— Calm down sweetie. Everything is fine. This is your new talent which has just revealed itself: pyrokinesia.

I breathe deeply, breathing in its smell, and the fire goes out by itself.

— OK. I'm i need to get trained to learn how to control it. I'm going to have to be careful.

— You? It is mainly me who better have to securing my rear. You can burn my ass if I get on your nerves!

I laugh and kiss him greedily. He's right, the idea may cross my mind, but I would never do anything with it. I love him like a crazy my authoritarian lion.

Extract Volume 3: Nate

— Don't cry my dears. Stay close to me. Everything will be alright.

— Mom, don't let go.

— Never Sam. I'll always be with you.

The man pushing them forward laughs in his beard. He already knows that the mother is lying without knowing it. They never leave families together. It's so much easier to manipulate and make parents submissive when they don't know what their offspring undergo. You might think that the shapeshifter is bad, but he is not. After all, they are masters of the world, or at least they will be soon. Fatels are only a means to an end, a sub—race without interest, except to serve them until death, a death which could happen soon if they do not obey. He is looking forward to it, as to him and to the other members of the clan, to plunge his teeth into the fresh flesh to revel in the warm blood of fatels and to feel the power invade him that he grunts in advance. He may even begin with this fatel who hold her girls with so much despair that she will be ready to endure everything to protect them. The child should not be more than five years old. These powers are embryonic, it's going to be easy to use her. Maybe even he will make her his mate later, when she is old and completely submissive to the clan. He heard that it was part of the plans of some packs to keep young children alive to rally them to the cause. It is a powerful and loyal beta. If he asks his alpha for this favor, he will certainly grant it.

From the same author

Ottawas series:

- — My Ottawa Lynx
- — My ottawa eagle
- —My ottawa beaver

The colors of the dragon

Fangs to My Blood

The colors of the dragon

Extract

Who has never imagined monsters in his closet or under his bed, or hidden behind a door or a dark corner, carpet in the shade, watching for our arrival in the dark to jump on us and mutilate us in an abominable way until does death ensue in excruciating pain? Well forget all about it because you are far from it. The reality is far worse than your mind can imagine. I have a talent, or rather, a curse. I see evil, the one who hides like the one who hangs out daylight among his future victims who suspect nothing, the one on Earth and beyond. Remember the most terrifying horror movie you've seen, with improbably shaped demons combining claws, fangs, venoms and awesome power, and you'll get a glimpse of the things I face on a regularly. Beside these monsters, fighting werewolves and vampires is like a health walk on Sunday. Not that I have time for that. I haven't walked in a park to get some fresh air for years, since my dear dad realized my potential and forever transformed my life into perpetual war.

www.ingramcontent.com/pod-product-compliance
Ingram Content Group UK Ltd.
Pitfield, Milton Keynes, MK11 3LW, UK
UKHW021933190726
13853UKWH00004B/1417

9 788835 406907